Three Knocks On the Wall

EVELYN SIBLEY LAMPMAN

PURPLE HOUSE PRESS
Kentucky

More captivating books from

EVELYN SIBLEY LAMPMAN

and Purple House Press

Bargain Bride
The Bounces of Cynthiann'
The City Under the Back Steps
The Shy Stegosaurus of Cricket Creek

Published by
Purple House Press
PO Box 787
Cynthiana, Kentucky 41031

Classic Living Books for Kids and Young Adults
purplehousepress.com

Summary: In a small Oregon town during World War I, a young girl befriends one of the mysterious people living next door in a house surrounded by a 10-foot wall.

ISBN 9781948959896

Three Knocks On the Wall

Chapter 1

THE DAY THAT I FIRST HEARD the knocks I'd walked home from school with Ethel Marie and Helen May Peterson. Not that I wanted to but they were better than nobody. They always took the back streets, which were quicker. I went to school that way, but usually I came home through town, which was more interesting. That morning Mama had told me I had to hurry straight home. She was making me a new dress for Miss Wallace's violin recital and she wanted to make sure that the hem was right. She said everybody would be staring at my hem, and if it dipped at the sides or went down in the front, people would talk about it.

It wasn't like Mama to be so particular about my clothes. She made sure I was clean and neat, but that was all. In the summer she even let me wear overalls when we went to the Point or some place really dirty. I don't know of any other girl in Maple Glen who got to wear boys' overalls. They always had to wear dresses and shoes and stockings, and the Peterson girls couldn't even go out in the sun without hats. So since Mama had made such a point of it, I thought I'd better hurry.

Ethel Marie and Helen May lived in the block beyond us in a big square house with a wide porch and a little tiny yard.

There were six houses on their block, and six more behind, with three at each side so they all had tiny yards. There wasn't even enough room for a Victory Garden. If the people wanted one, they had to plant it in their front flower beds.

I guess the Petersons really didn't need a bigger yard though because they never played in it anyway. They were too afraid of getting dirty. If they played outside it was on the porch, where they had tea parties for their dolls. I took one of my dolls to one of their parties a long time ago, but there wasn't anything but air in the teapot and not even a cookie on the plate because it might make crumbs. Helen May said dolls didn't really eat, so it didn't matter. But I never went to another of their parties. When Fay Phipps and I had tea parties we always had cookies and lemonade. We didn't play with dolls anymore, but I still had my dollhouse in my room. Sometimes when nobody was there I moved the furniture around and changed the dolls' dresses.

In our block there were only three houses and every one had a big yard, front and back. There weren't any houses behind us. The millrace ran along the back boundary and John Grant's hop yard was behind that. When we had a horse, which we did until we got our Model T Ford last year, we didn't have to carry water for her. She could just go down to the millrace and get a drink anytime she wanted. Now I guess the chickens drink there. I've seen their funny little three-toed claw marks in the mud at the shallow place.

The first house in the block belonged to Mrs. Hershy and her husband. She was a friend of mine, and I used to go visit her sometimes. I thought it was mean that people called her son, Ralph, a slacker just because he hadn't rushed to enlist in the army. I didn't like Ralph because he shot one of my cats once for killing their baby chickens, but I didn't like to see Mrs. Hershy hurt.

On the other side of our house was the Hutchinson place. You couldn't see it because they had built a wall ten feet high all around it, even in the back next to the millrace. There were round holes so the millstream could run through, but they weren't big enough so you could see anything.

Lots of people have fences around their yards, but this wasn't a fence. It was a real wall, and the boards went across instead of up and down and they were so tight there wasn't even a crack. Mama said she'd read in a book about the walled cities in Mexico. Every house in them was surrounded by a wall, too, so nobody could see in. This wall was like that, only it was built of wood not adobe.

There were two doors in the street side of the wall, one that was wide enough for the wood wagon to drive through each summer with Mrs. Hutchinson's winter firewood, and the other just a door to walk through. Not that anybody ever did except Mrs. Hutchinson or her daughter, Miss Rebecca. I know the doors were always locked, because I tried them once to see.

"I don't see how you can stand to live next to that crazy Mrs. Hutchinson," said Ethel Marie as we reached the wall on that particular day.

"Me, either," echoed Helen May. "She scares the daylights out of me."

"I don't ever see her," I pointed out reasonably. "A couple of times a week she goes down to her hardware store, and on Sunday she goes to church. The rest of the time she stays inside her wall."

"But what does she do in there?" asked Helen May curiously. "She and her daughter. They both must be crazy."

"Do you ever hear anything?" demanded Ethel Marie. "They must make some noise inside."

I couldn't remember hearing anything from the walled

enclosure except when the wood saw came to cut up Mrs. Hutchinson's firewood, but I didn't stop to think about it because it was then that I noticed the bird. It was a robin, lying perfectly still on the board sidewalk just ahead of us.

"Look!" I rushed ahead to stare down at the quiet little mound of feathers.

"Ugh!" Ethel Marie shivered and looked away.

"Is it dead?" Helen May came to stand next to us. "Poor little thing. I wonder what happened to it."

"It's dead all right," I assured them. I knew about such things.

"Probably a cat got it," said Ethel Marie. "That's one reason we don't have a cat. Besides all the hair and claw marks on the furniture, they're always bringing home dead birds and leaving them around."

"Only the feathers," I objected. "They eat the rest. It's their instinct to hunt."

The bird was intact. So far as I could see there wasn't a mark on it. Maybe it was very old and its heart had just stopped working.

"Well, find a stick and push it off the sidewalk," ordered Ethel Marie bossily. She's a year older than I am and in the eighth grade so she thinks she knows everything. "It would be awful for anybody to come along in the dark and step on it."

Instead I leaned down and picked it up. I could tell it hadn't been dead very long.

"How can you stand to touch it?" asked Helen May shuddering. "I couldn't."

I wondered why she felt that way, but then the Peterson girls were odd.

"What are you going to do with it?" she persisted. If she hadn't been such a scaredy cat and such a prissy, Helen May might have turned out all right. But you couldn't get her away from her older sister and Ethel Marie was poison.

"Take it home and give it a decent Christian burial, of course."

"Gracious!" said Ethel Marie sniffing. "I never heard of such a thing, Marty. Sometimes you're as bad as crazy old Mrs. Hutchinson. Come on, Helen May."

For a minute I was too mad to answer.

"Maybe I won't bury it after all," I yelled after them. "Maybe I'll take it home and cook it for supper. There's a meat shortage, or maybe you hadn't heard."

I could hear their scandalized gasps, but with their backs turned I couldn't see their faces. I was sorry about that. Ethel Marie had eyes that popped out a little, and it was fun to say things that made them pop out even farther.

I left the robin on the front steps of our house and hoped that Tiger wouldn't come along and find it before I got back. Inside, I told Mama my hands were dirty and I'd better wash them before I got dirt on my new dress. Since everybody knows that birds have lice, I used plenty of soap because I didn't want them crawling on me.

My recital dress was spread out on the bed waiting for me, and it was the prettiest thing I'd ever seen. It was pale blue and the whole skirt was tiny accordion pleats. It had a round neck, with an accordion pleated collar, edged with lace, and there was more accordion pleating around each puffed sleeve. I knew the sleeves would tickle my elbow, because they only came down that far, but I didn't say anything. You had to expect to suffer some if you looked that beautiful.

I could see why Mama was worried about the hem. The skirt was all finished, and she had to pin it to the waist and measure every inch to be sure it was even.

"This year you'll look just as nice as anyone. Maybe better." Mama looked up from the floor where she had to sit to do the pinning. "And your Aunt Gertrude won't be able to say a word."

"What did Aunt Gertrude say about me before?" I asked suspiciously.

"Not about you," Mama assured me quickly. "About me. She said I don't pay enough attention to your clothes. And I'll admit that last year your dress wasn't as fancy as some of the other girls in the recital, so maybe she's right."

Aunt Gertrude and Mama were always criticizing each other, so I didn't worry about it.

"Mama, is Mrs. Hutchinson really crazy?" I asked instead.

"She's odd. But she's not crazy. The hardware store has been making money since poor Harry died."

"But she doesn't run it. Ed Brown runs it for her. She only goes there a couple of times a week."

"I'm sure she has to approve what he does, however." Mama took out a pin and readjusted it.

"Why does she have that wall around her house?"

"I suppose she likes privacy. Some people do."

"How long has it been up?" I was sure Mama knew more about Mrs. Hutchinson than she was telling. "I can't remember when it wasn't there."

"No, I don't suppose you can. You were just a baby when the wall was built. Let's see, it was right after— The wall was built when you were a couple of years old. Mr. Hutchinson was alive then, and he had it built."

"But he's dead now. Why doesn't she tear it down?"

"She must like it, too." I could tell by the way she spoke that she wasn't going to say any more about the Hutchinsons' wall. Mama doesn't approve of gossip.

"There!" She patted me on the bottom. "Take it off very carefully and try not to loosen a single pin."

I was careful, but I hurried because I'd suddenly remembered the dead robin.

I got an almost-empty cornstarch box from the kitchen and dumped what was left in the sink. It looked about the right size for a coffin. When I tried it on the robin it was a tight squeeze, but I got it in. Then I got a shovel from Papa's tool shed and carried them both to my pet cemetery.

It was in our side yard and next to Mrs. Hutchinson's wall because that made it shady in the summer afternoons when the sun was hot. I thought the animals would like that.

It was a pretty big cemetery because we'd had lots of unfortunate accidents with pets. There were four cats buried there. Jiggs had died from having fits, and two little kittens were born dead, and Cleopatra just died and we never knew why. After Ralph Hershy shot the cat that caught his chickens, I would have buried her but I couldn't find the body and I was too mad at him to ask where it was. Then there was our old dog Ned, who died from old age, and my puppy Spot, who got distemper and never got over it. Besides that, there were two chickens. I've forgotten their names or what happened to make them die. And whenever I found a bird, as I had that day, I dug a hole and buried it as properly as I could.

I'd never been to a funeral because Mama didn't approve of children at funerals—she and Grandma and Aunt Gertrude used to argue about that—but I imagined it was a little like church. So after I'd dug the hole and put the cornstarch box in and covered it with dirt, I said a little prayer: "Dear God, This is one of your creatures. Please take care of it and send it straight to Bird Heaven. Amen."

Then I sang a song, probably *Jesus Loves Me* or *Onward Christian Soldiers* or something like that. When I finished I knelt down to put the big rock at the head of the little grave and it was then that I heard it.

There were three knocks on the boards of Mrs. Hutchinson's side of the wall right next to me.

For a minute I just stayed there, too petrified to move. The first thing I thought of was what Ethel Marie had said about Mrs. Hutchinson being crazy. Knocking on a wall like that was what a crazy person might do.

While I was sitting there, the knocks came again. One, two, three.

This time I decided to knock back. Even if she was crazy, there were heavy boards between us, and if worse came to worst I could run twice as fast as old Mrs. Hutchinson. So I stepped over the robin's grave and knocked three times on my side of the wall.

After a minute the knocks came again, only this time there were just two of them. I waited a minute, then I knocked back twice. After that Mrs. Hutchinson knocked four times, and that was just too much. It gave me a creepy feeling to have an old crazy woman knocking on the wall like that and I decided I'd better tell Mama.

Mama didn't believe me.

"Marty, I know you have a lively imagination, but you're old enough to learn to keep it under control." I could tell by her voice that she was exasperated. "Do you remember when you were little? You used to make up the most outrageous stories! Sometimes I think you did it just so you could get people upset, like the time you told me Grandma was burning all her feather beds in the back yard."

That had happened four years ago and I wished she'd forget about it, but she never would. I'd made up that story just to see the expression on Mama's face. For a whole month afterwards she and Papa wouldn't believe a thing I told them, even when it was the truth. So I didn't tell them stories anymore. Of course, I still said things to make people like Ethel Marie's eyes pop, but that was different.

"But Mama, it happened!" I insisted. "Come on and I'll show you."

"I'm working on your dress. And besides, it's preposterous to think that an old lady like Mrs. Hutchinson would play childish games."

"Then maybe it wasn't her," I insisted. "Maybe it was Miss Rebecca and she's crazy, too."

"*She,*" corrected Mama. "Maybe it wasn't *she*, not her. And I can promise you that it wasn't poor Rebecca either. She may be cowed, but she isn't crazy. No, Marty, I'm afraid your imagination has been running away with you again. No one knocked on the wall but you. Why don't you get your washcloth and knit a few rows? You'll never have it finished the rate you're going."

I didn't feel like working on the washcloth I was knitting for the Red Cross, so I went back outside and sat on the front step. Tiger was already there, enjoying a mouse he had caught. I hoped he'd finish it all and not leave the tail for me to sweep up as he usually did.

Then I sat up straight. Somebody passed by the gate in our high privet hedge. Although she didn't bother to speak I recognized Mrs. Hutchinson. So it couldn't have been her she—who was knocking on the wall.

I should have remembered it was Tuesday. Every Tuesday and Friday afternoon Mrs. Hutchinson spent a few hours at the hardware store she had inherited from her husband, probably making life miserable for poor Mr. Brown who ran it for her. When she came home her arms were always filled with big grocery sacks.

Once in a while, though, she probably forgot something,

for Miss Rebecca, all swaddled up in a long coat and a hat with a veil, would scuttle out the door in the wall. She always walked very fast, straight to Webster's Grocery Store. After a few minutes she'd come out with something in a smaller sack and hurry home without stopping to talk to anybody. I know because once I followed her to see where she was going.

The only other time the two went out was on Sunday when they both went to church. They always sat in the same pew, and afterwards they only waited long enough to shake hands with the preacher, then they came straight home. Mrs. Hutchinson would say, "How do you do," and, "Yes, it's a nice day," to people if they spoke to her. But Miss Rebecca didn't speak to anybody. She'd only nod and look down at the ground.

With Mrs. Hutchinson away, that narrowed the possibilities to one person. It had to be Miss Rebecca who had been knocking on the wall. I got up and told Tiger to be sure to finish off the mouse's tail. Then I picked a handful of flowers from the yard. That early in the spring there wasn't much blooming except some early crocus and a few snowdrops.

I carried them to my pet cemetery and counted them out over the graves. Every grave got at least one, and I gave the robin the two extra just to make it feel loved and cared for.

Then I knocked three times on the wall.

Nothing happened. I decided that when Miss Rebecca saw her mother come through the door, she must have run back into the house. It could only mean one thing. There wouldn't be any sounds from the other side except on Tuesdays and Fridays when Mrs. Hutchinson was gone.

Chapter 2

THE NEXT DAY WHEN I WENT TO SCHOOL, Mama gave me a little scrap of material from my new dress and told me to stop at Raubeck's Mercantile Store and buy a spool of buttonhole twist for the row of tiny buttons down the back. I would have gone through town anyway, but this gave me an excuse for taking my time.

I walked with Fay Phipps, who would have been my best friend if I had one, but I really didn't. I like a lot of people, but a lot of them I just put up with because I have to. Maybe there's something wrong with me, but that's the way it is.

Fay and I stopped at the corner of Main and Court Streets, as we always did, and looked at the war poster of Uncle Sam. No matter where you stood, on either side or straight ahead, his piercing blue eyes and his pointing finger were aimed straight at you.

There were a lot of these posters in places like the post office and courthouse. That year, 1917, when we got into war with Germany, they had sprouted up like dandelions.

"He doesn't mean us," said Fay in a troubled voice. Just to look at the poster made you feel guilty, as though you weren't doing enough for your country.

"We buy thrift stamps," I reminded her. "And when we have enough we turn them in for saving stamps. I guess when you're our age and a girl, that's all you can do."

"And knit for the Red Cross," remembered Fay. Her grandma had taught her and she knit almost as well as a grownup. "I just finished my third washcloth last night."

My first washcloth was so uneven and had so many dropped stitches that Mama had made me unravel it and start again. I decided it was better not to mention it.

"Anyway, my cousin Andy's in the army," I said, changing the subject. "He's in France fighting the Huns. And probably one in a family is all Uncle Sam really expects."

"Andy's only your cousin. My father's in the navy," Fay reminded me quickly as if I didn't know. "We don't know where he is because it's very secret, but we miss him terribly. Your cousin couldn't have got to France if it hadn't been for my father."

"You can't be sure of that." I didn't remind her that she only saw her father a couple of times a year even before the war. It would have hurt her feelings. Fay's mother died when she was three and she was being raised by her grandparents. Her father worked in Portland and only visited at Christmas and once during the summer. "Andy might have been on another ship."

"It's the same navy," she pointed out triumphantly.

"Well, my papa's on the draft board. He's too old to go to war, but he serves his country here at home. He says who should go and who shouldn't."

"Then he'd better get new spectacles," Fay told me snappishly. "That slacker Ralph Hershy's still hanging around town."

Much as I didn't like Ralph Hershy for shooting my cat, I had to agree with her. But I was mad that she inferred it was Papa's fault.

"I'm crossing here," I said stiffly.

Fay nodded and went on.

I headed for Papa's office, hoping he'd give me a nickel for candy.

I hadn't had any candy for a long time. I was supposed to save all my money to buy thrift stamps at school. A thrift stamp cost twenty-five cents and every Friday the teacher asked who was going to buy that week. She always reminded us that one thrift stamp would pay for a pair of socks for a soldier, or a gallon of gasoline for an airplane, or a knife, fork and spoon. You pasted your thrift stamps on a card, and when you had enough you could trade them for a war savings stamp worth five dollars. I generally bought a thrift stamp every week, and I didn't want to miss. That's why I planned to ask Papa for an extra nickel.

The war we were in was a terrible thing. I didn't understand it very well. We didn't have it in our history class because it was going on right now and wasn't history.

All the countries in Europe were fighting, and it had been going on more than three years by the time we got into it. People said it was started by Germany because Kaiser Bill (his real name was Wilhelm or something, but we always called him Bill) wanted to conquer the world like Alexander the Great.

He had a big army, all trained, and first he sent it into some place called the Balkans, then into little Belgium. You heard a lot about the poor, starving Belgian babies and how the German soldiers liked to run them through with their bayonets. Mama claimed you couldn't believe all the war stories and that part probably wasn't true, but that's what people said.

Some of the countries in Europe were helping Kaiser Bill, but the big ones, France, Great Britain and Italy, were against him and they called themselves the Allies. Japan thought this was a good time to attack China, because their island was small and they needed more land. Pretty soon almost everybody was fighting somebody.

We probably wouldn't have got into it except that Kaiser Bill had a lot of U-Boats (I think the U stood for Underwater) and pretty soon they began sinking American ships. President Wilson said we couldn't put up with that and Congress finally agreed with him. The first thing we knew we were at war, too. Then it was called the World War.

My cousin Andy, Aunt Gertrude and Uncle Horace's son, who is eleven years older than I am, was at college, but he and his friend Glen French quit right in the middle of the year and came back to join Maple Glen's National Guard. Both Mama and Papa thought he should have waited for June, but Aunt Gertrude and Uncle Horace were as proud as two peacocks. Andy trained for several months, first in Oregon, finally someplace else, and then he was sent overseas. For the first time Aunt Gertrude began to worry, but I didn't. I knew Andy and Glen could take care of themselves. They always had. They were probably having fun.

Things were different at home though, once we got into the war. We had to conserve food, so we could send a lot to our soldiers, and all the ladies worked a day a week at the Red Cross, cutting and rolling bandages. In their spare time they knitted sweaters and helmets and socks, and people my age were supposed to knit those awful washcloths out of slippery cotton yarn. Every house, like Aunt Gertrude and Uncle Horace's, that had a boy in the service hung a flag with a blue star in the front window, as many stars as there were soldiers in the family. If the star was gold, you knew that soldier had been killed. There weren't very many of these. Not at first.

Sugar was scarce and we were supposed to have victory

gardens and grow our own food. We had a big one, and that's when Papa bought the chickens because there was plenty of room in the barnyard and eggs were expensive—forty-nine cents a dozen.

When the hens were laying well, Mama put some up in a crock filled with Egg Saver, which was a powder she bought at the drug store and mixed with water. When the hens stopped laying, which they did from time to time, she always had eggs for cooking or you could eat them scrambled. They weren't any good fried or boiled because the yolks were runny.

I guess they must have shipped lots of wheat flour to the soldiers because it was hard to get, and for every pound you bought you had to buy as much graham or rice or rye flour. They didn't allow you to have extra flour on hand either. People who did were supposed to turn it in to the government. If they didn't they were called hoarders. Papa read us a story from the paper about some people who hoarded and they were sent to jail and had to pay a big fine besides.

They were always having meatless days when the butcher shops were closed, and you were supposed to eat things like macaroni or eggs. But all in all, except for the candy, it wasn't too bad, and everybody said that now the American doughboys were there the war would soon be over.

Papa wasn't in his office when I got there, and George Rimshaw, who did the typing, said he was across the street at the courthouse.

"They're trying that forger today," he explained. "Won't be much of a trial though. Ought to be over any minute. It's an open and shut case. What you want your pa for? Looking for a nickel?"

"It would be nice. I've been putting all my pennies into thrift stamps, and it's been so long since I had any candy I've almost forgotten what it tastes like."

He nodded sympathetically.

"War's hard on everybody, even children."

I remembered that Mama was waiting for the buttonhole twist so I decided not to wait for Papa. When I went back down the street past the war poster I thought about George Rimshaw. Uncle Sam didn't need him. One of his legs was about four inches shorter than the other, and even with built-up shoes he walked with a lurch. I wondered what he thought when he saw the poster. He probably wanted to be a soldier and it must make him sad to think he couldn't.

Raubeck's Mercantile Store wasn't crowded. There was only one customer, Miss Edna Pope, and she was matching thread too. I took Mama's sample of material from my pocket and stood back waiting until she had finished.

I had never talked to Miss Edna, but I knew all about her. Mrs. Hershy had told me one day when I was calling on her. Miss Edna's mama had run away and when she came home it was very plain she was going to have a baby. Her parents took her in even though people said she had never been married. She died when Miss Edna was born and the Popes raised the baby. Miss Edna went to school at Maple Glen, which couldn't have been easy because everybody knew, and when she graduated she hung out a dressmaking sign.

At first nobody came to her, but she entered a dress in the county fair and it won first prize. A lady from Salem bought it and before long a lot of Salem ladies were driving fifteen miles just to get her to make their dresses. When the Maple Glen ladies heard about that, some of them went to Miss Edna, but she wouldn't always take them. She told Mrs. Pickering that she was too fat to be wearing a pattern of great big splashy roses and that she'd have nothing to do with it. Mrs. Pickering was awfully mad, but she couldn't do anything about it. Then Mrs. Dawes took her some material and Miss

Edna said it was shoddy and not worth the price of making up. That got around town pretty fast.

Then Mrs. Buchanan asked her if she'd make Myra's wedding gown and bridesmaid dresses and Miss Edna said yes, providing she could help pick out the material. Myra's wedding was the talk of Maple Glen, and after that it was considered very elegant to have a dress made by Edna Pope. People always bragged about it because she charged a lot.

While I was staring at her back, she turned around and smiled.

"Did you want thread, too, Marty?" she asked. Her face was very plain until she smiled. Then it changed. "I didn't mean to monopolize the rack. Come over and we can share it."

"I want buttonhole twist," I told her shyly. "Blue, like this." I showed her my sample.

Miss Edna took it from me and felt it carefully. I held my breath, hoping she wouldn't say something bad about it.

"Good quality," she said approvingly. "Is it for you?"

"My recital dress." Then before I knew it I was telling her all about the dress, how it was made and how hard Mama had worked to get the skirt even. She was very easy to talk to and not mean at all like some of the ladies said she was.

"I'm sure it's very pretty," she said when I'd finished. "Now let's look for your buttonhole twist. If you can't get the exact match, and you hardly ever can from Raubeck's stock, you must get the twist a shade darker than the material. If it's lighter it will show up more."

She helped me find the right shade and told Mr. Raubeck to ring mine up first.

"I have several spools to buy. Marty has only one," she explained.

As Mr. Raubeck took my quarter and put it with the sales slip into the container that ran on wires up to the cashier in the balcony, I wondered how she knew my name. I didn't like to ask.

"Do you sew, Marty?" asked Miss Edna. "Doll clothes maybe?"

"I'm not very good at it," I admitted. I didn't like to explain that when you're twelve you weren't expected to play with dolls.

"Sewing takes practice," she told me. "I have lots of scraps. They're left over from my sewing. Small pieces, of course. Why don't you stop by my house someday and I'll give them to you? Maybe I can even help you make a doll dress. But be sure to ask your mother first."

The little container with my slip and change slid down the wires and Mr. Raubeck detached it. He put my spool of twist in a small bag and handed me a dime.

"Fifteen cents for a spool of buttonhole twist is highway robbery, Henry Raubeck," said Miss Edna. "There's not that much thread on a spool, even if it is silk."

"It's the war," he told her. "Besides, I hear you've raised your prices, too, Miss Pope."

"People don't have to come to me," she said, shrugging her shoulders. "I charge what the market will bear."

When I got home I told Mama about my conversation with Miss Edna.

"Poor soul," said Mama. "I expect she's lonely. I think it would be fine for you to call on her, Marty, and if she offers to help you with your sewing it's even better. Goodness knows, I can't get you to take small stitches. Maybe she can."

"You don't care that she's...that her mother wasn't married?"

"It's none of my concern." Mama frowned. "And it certainly isn't Edna's fault. I can't imagine where you heard that old story anyway. It happened a long time ago and it's much better forgotten."

"Yes, ma'am," I agreed, and went outside because if I'd stayed I knew she'd give me a lecture on the evils of gossiping.

I stood on the porch wondering what to do until supper-time. Only the Peterson girls and I lived on this side of Main Street. There were several boys, but they didn't count.

For a minute I stared at the Hutchinsons' wall. Even a game of knock with crazy Miss Rebecca would have been fun, but it was Wednesday and Mrs. Hutchinson would be home. Finally I went to my room and rearranged the furniture in my dollhouse.

Chapter 3

I WAS TOO BUSY to play knock on the wall games with crazy Miss Rebecca. I had Miss Wallace's recital to worry about.

I played *Humoresque,* and Mama and Papa said I was the best on the program. Of course, they were prejudiced, but even Grandma, who had driven in from the farm and was spending the night at Aunt Gertrude's, said I did well enough, and she was always pretty sparing with her praise. Aunt Gertrude said my blue accordion-pleated dress was very appropriate, every bit as nice as Edna Pope could make, and why didn't Mama always pay that much attention to my clothes?

Naturally that started another argument, with Mama saying that it was enough that I had a bath every day and was clean and used correct grammar. I didn't have to be a clotheshorse too. Then Grandma, who had crossed the plains in a covered wagon where there wasn't much water to wash in, claimed a bath every day was wasteful, besides being hard on the skin, and before we knew it the three of them were arguing like they always did, and everybody forgot about my recital. Especially me. I was only glad it was over.

Over the weekend it began to rain. February had been nice, with occasional showers and in between there had been pale blue skies with bouncy white clouds like the baby lambs that were appearing in the fields outside of town. Then all of a sudden the blue was gone, swallowed up by a thick gray tent dripping with water. It rained almost all the time, and since she was nearly as old as Mama, I knew that Miss Rebecca wouldn't want to come out and squat in the mud next to the wall, so I stayed away, too. Besides, I was pretty busy.

Mama had got all fired up with the compliments on my accordion-pleated recital dress, and she decided it was time to make my spring clothes. She sewed for me twice a year, in February or March and again in August, just before school started. In winter I always had two wool dresses for school. In the spring I had two cotton dresses and a new pair of overalls. Of course I always had a Sunday school dress, too.

Mama picked out the patterns, either from the Delineator or Butterick books in Raubeck's Mercantile Store, but I got to pick out the material. This year, because of the war, there wasn't as much as usual to choose from and Mama said the prices were a scandal. Percale that should be ten cents a yard was up to eighteen cents, and twelve-and-a-half-cent gingham cost twenty-two cents a yard. But there was nothing we could do but pay for it. I'd grown since fall and I had to have new Ferris waists with long elastic supporters to hold up my stockings, but we didn't buy shoes. Papa always wanted to do that. He made a big fuss about buying my shoes, poking at my feet to make sure there was plenty of room. He said corns were a terrible thing and he never wanted a child of his to be subjected to them.

It took a couple of weeks for Mama to sew all these things, and I had to come straight home nearly every day to try them on. But it really didn't matter because it rained on and off every day. About the time she finished, the rain stopped.

"I knew it would," said Mama. "The equinox is over. The

sun has started north again. We can expect some nice weather now that the equinoxial storm has ended."

I guess she was right. It really smelled like spring when I started for Sunday school the next morning. There were fat knobs on the branches of the maple trees just quivering to burst into leaves. The grass was washed green and rain-polished with a few purple and yellow crocus scattered here and there across the yard and some half-opened daffodils in the bed beside the privet hedge. It was a day to be outside, not shut up in the church basement, so I was glad when Sunday school was over.

Mama was just coming into church as I left. She generally went every Sunday, though Papa only went Christmas or Easter when I was on the program. His parents died before I was born so I never knew them, but I guess they were very religious. When he was a boy. Papa had to go to church three times on Sunday and once during the week. He said if you counted up the times, it would make up for the rest of his life. It made it nice for me though, because there would be someone at home when I got back.

I met Mrs. Hutchinson and Miss Rebecca coming down the street. They were hurrying along lickety-split. I said good morning and Mrs. Hutchinson mumbled something, but Miss Rebecca just bobbed her head the way she always did. You'd have thought she'd look at me after all that knocking on the wall, but she didn't.

Papa was putting on his hip boots when I got home so I knew he was going out to the barnyard. He looked up and smiled before he started tugging at the boot again.

Papa isn't exactly handsome and he isn't very tall, but you don't think of that. You think, "Now here's somebody I could take my troubles to," and a lot of people do. You could hardly carry on a conversation with him walking down the street because every person you met smiled and spoke to him and about half of them stopped and wanted to talk. He has twinkly blue eyes, a sort of big nose, and the only hair he has left is a fringe around his baldness but that doesn't matter. On his last birthday he said he had reached half a hundred years. I suppose it's true, but you don't think of that either. Papa's never changed all the years I've known him.

"All that rain's washed limbs and debris down the millrace," he told me, standing up and reaching for his heavy sweater. "It's jammed up like a beaver dam against the Hutchinsons' wall, and I'll have to clean it out. Fool woman, anyway!"

"Is Mrs. Hutchinson crazy?" I asked quickly. I hadn't thought to ask Papa about her before.

"Let's just say she's got some mighty peculiar ideas."

"How about Miss Rebecca?"

"That milksop!" He snorted as he went out the back door. "If she'd had any gumption she would have kept on going that time she left."

The door slammed behind him and I realized that was a little piece of information I'd never heard before. Miss Rebecca must have tried to leave home, but for some reason she had come back. I couldn't imagine timid, rabbit-like Miss Rebecca daring to leave home without permission. I wondered what else Papa could tell me.

I got into my overalls and an old coat and squeezed my shoes into black rubbers. Then I crossed the backyard and swung open the wire gate to plow through the muddy barnyard to the millrace.

Papa was right. So many limbs and branches had washed down with the heavy rains that they were piled halfway up the side of the Hutchinsons' wall. They had choked the holes cut for the current to flow through and the water had overflowed the banks and was three feet up into our barnyard. Papa was prying limbs loose with a pitchfork and hauling them up into the middle of the yard to burn. I could tell by his face that he was in no mood to talk, so I didn't stay. Instead I decided I'd visit my pet cemetery and make sure all the graves were safe.

The cemetery needed raking, since a lot of brown leaves had blown up against the wall and several of the grave marker stones which I had stuck in upright had blown over. I started making it presentable again.

It was nice working in the sunshine even though my feet were sopping wet clear through the rubbers. I sang to myself as I set up stones and scraped away dead leaves. Since it wasn't a funeral, I didn't have to sing Sunday school songs. I could sing popular songs, which was more fun.

I'd just finished "K-K-K-Katie" and was starting on "Over There" when I heard it. *Knock knock knock* came from the other side of the Hutchinsons' wall.

I was so surprised that I sat right down on the wet ground. Church wasn't over, and with my own eyes I'd seen both Mrs. Hutchinson and Miss Rebecca going there. Miss Rebecca must have come back.

The three knocks came again, and after a minute I got up and went over to the wall.

"What do you want?" I shouted.

Nobody answered but there were three more knocks.

I thought about getting Papa, but he was mad enough at the Hutchinsons for walling over the millrace, so I didn't. Instead I knocked back three times.

Immediately there were two knocks from the other side.

The whole thing was very silly. Two people knocking on a wall when all we had to do was raise our voices a little to be heard.

"Who are you?" I called again, and the only answer was three more knocks. If only the boards hadn't been fitted so tightly together! I couldn't even find a crack to peek through.

"Listen," I called. "I'm not going to get splinters in my hands, even if you want to. I'll talk and you can knock. Knock once for yes and twice for no. Do you understand?"

There was a single knock on the wall, and I felt very proud of myself. Miss Rebeca and I would play Twenty Questions. All I'd have to remember was to ask questions that could be answered by yes or no.

"Are you female?" I asked, starting easy.

As I expected, there was a single knock.

"Do you live in the house next door?"

The answer was yes.

"Did you go to church today?"

She knocked no. I wished I could ask her how she had managed to get away from her mother, but that was impossible. I'd have to find out some other way.

"Did you say you were feeling sick?"

There were two knocks, so Miss Rebecca must have given her mother another reason and I couldn't think of any.

"Do you know my name?"

She knocked that she did.

"And I know yours, too," I told her. "It's Miss Rebecca, isn't it?"

There were two knocks on the wall.

"You have to tell the truth," I told her angrily. "It's not fair if you don't. You are Miss Rebecca."

This time the two knocks were very loud.

"But only Mrs. Hutchinson and Miss Rebecca live next door," I insisted.

Again there were two knocks. Whoever was on the other side was trying to make me believe that a third person lived inside the walled-in house. And I knew better.

"What kind of game are you playing, Marty," called Papa. He had finished clearing the choked-up millrace and was crossing the backyard. "You're talking to yourself."

"No, I'm not. Papa. Come here. Quick!"

At last I would have proof of what I had heard. He had arrived right in the midst of the knocking. When he heard it for himself he would tell Mama that I wasn't making up stories again.

As soon as he was close enough, I spoke to the person on the other side.

"This is my Papa. He's a very nice man. Have you seen him, too?"

From the other side of the wall there was nothing but silence. In desperation I knocked on it myself. There was no answer.

"It seems rather a futile game," said Papa smiling. "But then I don't pretend to understand what goes on in a little girl's head. Church must be over by now. Do you think we ought to get some of this mud off us before your mama gets home?"

"I guess so," I agreed. Somehow I knew there would be no more knocks on the wall that day.

Chapter 4

Everybody in Maple Glen has Sunday dinner at two o'clock. As soon as she got home from church, Mama began getting ours ready. She built up the fire and put the boiled chicken over the hottest part of the stove. I set the table, then I went back to the kitchen.

"I met Mrs. Hutchinson and Miss Rebecca hurrying to church," I told her. "They must have been late."

"They were a little." Mama dropped dough into the pot of boiling chicken. In twelve minutes it would turn into dumplings so light you didn't have to chew them if you didn't want to. "They came in during the first hymn."

"Did they sit where you could see them?" I asked, trying not to sound too interested.

"Did they...I don't remember where they sat." Mama popped the lid on the kettle and looked at her watch, "Why? What's so important about where Rebecca and her mother sat?"

"I just wondered. Their regular pew is right up front. I wondered, since they were late, if it was filled when they got there."

"Oh." I hadn't had much time to think about it, but my

answer must have been a good one. Anyway it satisfied her. "No, come to think of it, their regular seats were filled today. They must have had to sit somewhere else. I didn't notice."

That meant that Miss Rebecca could have made an excuse to her mother and sneaked out at any time! I didn't realize that I was smiling at the way I'd found her out until I saw Mama was looking at me curiously.

"That must have made Mrs. Hutchinson mad," I suggested quickly.

"I don't imagine she was too happy." Even Mama smiled, and I stopped thinking about Miss Rebecca long enough to think how pretty my mama was. She had long black hair done up in a knot on top of her head and eyes the color of brown pansies. She was a little plump, with dimples in her elbows and another in one cheek that only came out when she smiled. "The Hutchinsons have occupied that same pew ever since I can remember. By now I imagine she believes she owns it."

I knew it wasn't safe to talk much more about the Hutchinsons or Mama might ask me why I was so interested. I decided not to ask Papa, either, because I'd just remembered I had a much better source of information. Mrs. Hershy, our next door neighbor on the other side, would tell me everything she knew or had ever heard. Mrs. Hershy loved to gossip.

As soon as the dishes were done I went over to her house. A couple of boys I knew were coming down the street, and when they saw me turn into the Hershy walk, one of them yelled at me.

"You shouldn't go in there, Marty Burnham. Don't you know a slacker lives there?"

"I'm going to see Mrs. Hershy. She's no slacker. And Mr. Hershy is too old to go to war. He's as old as my grandpa."

"It's not them. It's their son, Ralph. He's the slacker. Too yellow to fight for his country."

By now the boys had caught up with me and I stopped. They were practically shouting and even though the door was closed, I was afraid Mrs. Hershy would hear.

"You shut up, Freddy Taylor!" I whispered, partly for Mrs. Hershy's sake and partly for my own. I was almost sure Mama was safely in the house, but she could have come outside after I left. I had two vocabularies, one for school, one for home, and I was careful not to mix them. If my friends ever heard me say, "It was I," they would have been as horrified as Mama would have been to hear, "Shut up."

"Make me," dared Freddy.

"You'll be sorry if you don't," I warned, not even stopping to think what I could do to make him sorry.

A couple of years ago I would have really lit into him, but now I was too old. The last time I'd come home with a black eye, Mama had sat me down and explained that ladies didn't have fist fights with gentlemen. And she didn't ever want to hear of me doing it again.

"Oh, come on, Fred," urged Orville Dunn. "What do you care if Marty gets slimy slacker juice on herself?"

He and Freddy continued on down the street and in a minute were hidden by the tall privet hedge that marked our property line. I went on up the walk and knocked on the door. The instant Mrs. Hershy opened it, both boys jumped out from behind the hedge.

"Slimy slacker! Slimy slacker!" they shouted, and I stood there, mortified, because I should have guessed what they'd planned to do.

Mrs. Hershy pretended not to hear them.

"Why Marty, come in, honey. Come in," she urged and shut the door firmly as soon as I did.

"We'd best go out to the kitchen," she told me in a whisper. "William's having his after-dinner nap."

Mr. Hershy was stretched full-length on the lounge against the wall in the sitting room. He was snoring loudly, and every time he let out a breath his white beard wiggled in a fascinating sort of way. I didn't think there was much danger of waking him, but I happily followed his wife to the kitchen. It was my favorite room in the house.

"There's still coffee in the pot," said Mrs. Hershy hospitably. "You'll have a cup, Marty?"

I said yes. The only time I got to drink coffee was at the Hershys. I wasn't allowed to have it at home because it might stunt my growth. I couldn't drink Coca-Cola either, because it was supposed to have cocaine in it, but nobody ever offered me any of that. I guess it was too expensive, five cents for just a little glass.

Mrs. Hershy got a couple of cups and saucers from the dresser and with the folds of her apron over her hand she moved the granite coffeepot forward on the wood cookstove.

"I'll just het it up a bit," she explained. "It's a sin to put cold coffee in decent stomachs."

While the coffee was reheating, I sniffed the familiar aroma of Mrs. Hershy's kitchen. I don't know why, but everybody's kitchen smells different. Mrs. Hershy's smelled of scouring with her homemade soap. It was a clean smell, but a little sweet, too, and if I'd been blindfolded I'd have known where I was the minute I came in the room.

"I don't know why people are so mean about Ralphie," said Mrs. Hershy after a minute. She kept her back turned to me, and I wondered if she were crying.

"Some people are just born mean," I told her uncomfortably.

"It isn't like Ralphie didn't want to do his part." She

seemed to be talking to herself, not to me. "But he's never been strong. He's not a well boy."

I'd never heard of Ralph Hershy being sick before. He'd always looked like a big strong man to me. But I didn't say anything. Instead I sat there, looking around the immaculate kitchen, with the big black wood stove giving off its comforting heat and occasionally a crackling pop when the flame found a knot of pitch, at the cupboard with its pierced tin sides, the rows of shelves filled with assorted crockery and the closed cupboards beneath for Mrs. Hershy's pots and pans. From where I was sitting at the center table I could look out the window at our own backyard next door, and beyond that the Hutchinsons' wall, which blocked the view farther down the street.

"There, I reckon that's hotted up enough." Mrs. Hershy recovered herself and lifted the gray granite coffee pot from the stove. She filled our cups, then pushed the sugar bowl and a cream pitcher across the table.

"Help yourself," she invited.

I remembered we were expected to save for the war so I only had two spoonsful of sugar in my coffee, though I'd rather have had three, but I made up for it with lots of cream. I really don't like coffee, so lots of cream and sugar helps to hide the taste.

Before she sat down Mrs. Hershy opened a drawer and pulled out a folded square of shiny tinfoil.

"This come off a package of tea," she said, handing it to me. "I saved it for you."

"Thank you. It's the nice, heavy kind, too. Better than gum wrappers."

Everybody, especially children, saved tinfoil for the war. I don't know what people did with it after we turned it in, but it was probably something important. We stripped the tinfoil off gum wrapper papers and everything else we could find and rolled it into a hard ball. Mine was as big as an egg, but a boy at school had one the size of a baseball. The teacher said his was ready to turn in.

"Did you go to church today?" Mrs. Hershy smiled at me over the rim of her coffee cup. You didn't have to see her mouth to know that she was smiling. Her whole face sort of crinkled up.

"I went to Sunday school. But Mama went to church. Mrs. Hutchinson and Miss Rebecca went too, but they were late. Somebody else was sitting in their pew when they got there."

Mrs. Hershy put down her cup and leaned toward me, her elbows on the table. Her blue eyes got very bright. There was nothing she liked as well as a little bit of gossip.

"I bet Phoebe Hutchinson was fit to be tied," she declared delightedly. "Did she say anything?"

"Not that I know of," I admitted. Mama wouldn't know about anything like that and if she did she wouldn't repeat it.

"I bet a cookie she did. To the preacher or somebody. She's getting old, you know, and set in her ways."

Mrs. Hershy was about the same age as Mrs. Hutchinson but I didn't like to point that out. I'd only brought up the story because it would make a good way to get into what I wanted to talk about.

"Why did they build that wall around their house?" I asked.

"I never could find out," she admitted sadly. "Though I tried, of course. Even asked Phoebe Hutchinson herself, but she closed up tighter than a sealed pickle jar. All she'd ever say was that they wanted their privacy. But there had to be another reason."

"Could there be somebody else living there besides her and Miss Rebecca?" I didn't for one minute think there was, but after all that knocking this morning I might as well be sure.

As I expected, Mrs. Hershy shook her head.

"Just the two of them ever since poor Harry passed on. Two people rattling around in a great big house and all that yard to take care of. Not that I doubt for a minute that Phoebe Hutchinson hasn't got a nice garden. She always did have a green thumb, and she's got Rebecca to do the spading and weeding. Myself, I can't get down no more to weed and neither can William, but we've got Ralphie. That's really why he doesn't go to war, you know. He looks after us." Her soft, wrinkled face grew glum again and I hurried to get her mind off Ralphie's problems.

"I wonder why Miss Rebecca stays there. Didn't she ever want to get married?"

"Rebecca never had no beaus that I remember," said Mrs. Hershy, instantly diverted. "I guess Harry and Phoebe kept the young men at a distance. Only time I ever saw one shine up to Rebecca was at that circus."

"What circus?" I prompted, for she had stopped speaking, her face puckered up in thought.

"That's what I'm trying to remember, child," she told me reproachfully. "Was it Sells-Floto or Barnum and Bailey? Well, no matter. Harry couldn't leave the store and Phoebe was laid up with a swollen jaw. Bad tooth. She had it out the next day or the day after. Well, anyway, Rebecca went to the matinee with the Parson girl, only she never went inside. Spent the whole time talking with one of the roustabouts that put up the tent and take it down. Alma Parson went in and saw the whole performance, but Rebecca just sat outside with that roustabout. I seen her myself when I went in and she was still there, jabbering away, when I come out. No, that's the only time I remember that Rebecca came anywhere close to having a beau, and you can't hardly count that. She must have been about seventeen or eighteen then, and hasn't had a beau in all those years or since."

I did some quick arithmetic and decided Miss Rebecca wasn't as old as Mama after all. Maybe it was the way she dressed that made her look that way. She had to be around thirty-something now. But that was still too old to be playing games.

"Didn't she go away for a while?" I asked as patiently as I could.

"Yes. Yes, she did. Pretty soon after that, too. The Hutchinsons never told anybody beforehand that she was going to visit relatives in Seattle, either. They just said she was gone. She stayed quite a spell. Almost a year as I recollect. Then Phoebe went up to fetch her back, and after she'd stayed for a little visit herself they both come home. But there was something funny about it…"

"What?"

"Nobody could figure out how they got here," said Mrs. Hershy thoughtfully. "I asked Phoebe, but she just talked around the subject and I never could pin her down. Everybody knew that Harry Hutchinson wouldn't drive his car on the road after dark, so he couldn't have gone in to Salem to fetch them from the train. And they wasn't on the little gasoline car that makes connections to Maple Glen so they didn't come by that. And nobody remembered seeing a strange automobile or wagon that could have brought them. They was just here. Here behind that ugly wall of theirs, and here they've been ever since."

"The wall was up then?"

"Yes," said Mrs. Hershy positively. "It was there when they got back, but it wasn't there when Rebecca went away. So it was built while she was gone. Must have been a dreadful shock to her, poor thing, to find it. Like living in a prison."

"Mama says it was built when I was a baby."

"That's right," agreed Mrs. Hershy beaming. She got up to fill our coffee cups again.

"The Petersons must have had company for a meal last week," she told me, sitting down again. "Mrs. Peterson was late getting her wash on the line. Didn't get it hung till Wednesday, and there was two extra table napkins. Did one of the girls happen to tell you who they had?"

"No, they didn't," I confessed sadly. It would have been nice to be able to satisfy her curiosity.

But suddenly I understood why Mama always sent our laundry to Yuey Kim. Not only were our clotheslines plainly visible from the street but they were in sight of Mrs. Hershy's kitchen windows.

Mama didn't gossip about other people, and she didn't want them gossiping about her either.

Chapter 5

I TRIED KNOCKING ON THE WALL on both Tuesday and Friday afternoons when I was sure Mrs. Hutchinson was in the hardware store, but there wasn't any answer. On Sunday I hung around outside the church for quite a while waiting for Miss Rebecca to sneak out. When I was sure she wasn't coming, I went home and didn't bother with the wall. I figured there wouldn't be any use in it with no one to knock back. Anyway, Miss Rebecca was probably tired of her little game.

Henry Riggs, who did our spading, had been there that week and had turned over the vegetable bed in back and Mama's flower beds in the front, so after dinner we all went outside to set things out. Everything was late that year because of the rain lasting so long.

"Henry probably should have spaded my beds first," said Mama, getting down on her knees and reaching for the trowel. "Then I could have taken care of this yesterday. A lot of people are going to think I'm breaking the Sabbath. Some of them even eat cold food so they won't have to cook on Sunday. This will really shock them."

"You could wait till tomorrow, Bea," Papa reminded her, and I could tell by his voice he was teasing.

"No," she decided. "The ground's just right. By tomorrow it could start raining again."

I helped Mama plant her seeds. She had everything all planned out. The marigolds went in a straight line down the walk. Poppy seed I sprinkled in a round patch that Hen Riggs had dug, and I took special care with that because I loved those poppies best of all. They were practically all colors except blue and their petals were thin as tissue paper. They only lasted a day or so, but they looked pretty on the graves in my pet cemetery. Then we planted Baby's Breath and Cosmos and a lot of other things.

We couldn't plant nasturtiums because they took a poor soil and ours was too rich. When he wasn't being a judge, Papa was a lawyer, and some of his clients paid their bills with loads of manure. It happened every year and we probably had the richest soil of anyone in Maple Glen. For a few days, after Hen Riggs spread it around, we had the smelliest, too.

Mama's wallflowers had frozen out last winter, and I was bending over planting new seed next to the chimney when she called to me.

"Marty, go get your father. He has callers."

There were three Indians coming down our boardwalk. The leader was a man with braids swinging below his big black hat. His face was sort of lined, not with wrinkles, but as though he always wore the same expression and the lines had just settled there. He wore white man's clothes, a wrinkled jacket with baggy pants that didn't match and a white shirt without a collar. Behind him was a younger man, a boy really, who looked so much like the first I knew it had to be his son. And behind him was a girl about my age. She had on a calico dress that wasn't too clean and her black hair had either been blown by the wind or she hadn't bothered to comb it when she left home. She was barefoot and she looked scared.

I put down my package of seeds and raced around back to get Papa. He was planting radishes, but he stopped the minute I told him about the visitors. He didn't look surprised, and I wasn't either. Indians from the reservation were always stopping by our house to talk with him. The only surprise was the girl. Indian men didn't usually bring their daughters with them when they came.

The three were sitting in a row on the porch bench when we got back and Papa went up to the older man with his hand out.

"*Klahowya,* Tom," he said. Papa had learned Chinook jargon because some of the reservation people didn't like to talk English.

Indian Tom shook Papa's hand and said something I couldn't understand. Papa shook hands with the son and spoke to the girl. She didn't answer. She just covered her mouth with her hand and giggled.

"Marty," Papa turned to me. "This is Agnes. Why don't you take her out to your swings and the two of you can play while I talk with her father?"

"All right," I agreed. It would be nice to have someone new to play with. Sundays were always boring because most kids were expected to stay home with their folks. "Come on, Agnes."

Agnes didn't seem to want to come. She just ducked her head and kept giggling behind her hand all the time Papa was explaining about my swings.

"Why don't you get a few cookies, Marty?" suggested Mama, who had taken over with the wallflower seeds. "They might break the ice."

So I went inside to get them and when I came back Agnes got right up and followed me to the swings.

I have two swings. One is ordinary rope and the other is

in a sort of wooden frame with two seats facing each other. It doesn't go very high, but when I was smaller I used to play train on it. I don't use it much anymore, except that it makes a good seat when I'm reading. But that's the one Agnes liked best. Maybe she'd never seen one before. We sat facing each other, eating our cookies.

"My name's Marty," I began. "It's Martha really, but nobody ever calls me that."

She looked at me shyly but didn't answer.

"Agnes is a nice name." I lied when I said it because it's not a name I've ever cared for. "Do you have another name, too?"

"Ten-as-pish," she told me.

That sounded as bad as Agnes, even in her soft little voice.

"That's nice." I tried to sound more enthusiastic than I felt. "What does it mean?"

"Little Fish," she told me, and this time there was no disguising the pride in her voice.

Oh, well. Names weren't important. And probably Marty sounded ugly to her, too.

"Do you come to Maple Glen often?" I asked.

"No. This is first time I come. First time off reservation." Under the influence of the cookies and the gentle motion of the swing her shyness was finally melting.

I could hardly believe my ears. Maple Glen isn't much, maybe three thousand people, but to someone who'd never seen any town at all it must really be something.

"Did you drive through downtown? Did you see the stores and the courthouse?"

"No." She shook her head, and I could tell she was disappointed. "My father came only here. He has business."

"Well, he'll probably drive down Main Street and let you look around before you leave," I reassured her.

"No. He will hurry home. We have stock to feed."

I jumped out of the swing, which set it to shaking, and Agnes hung onto the arms of her seat in alarm. I couldn't let that happen. Poor little girl. Driving fifteen miles here and fifteen back and not even a glimpse of Main Street.

"You wait here," I told her quickly. "I'll be right back."

Mama was very sympathetic when I explained about Agnes.

"Poor little thing," she said. "Tell Papa. Let him ask her father if Agnes can walk downtown with you. I'll get you each a penny to spend for candy. But after you do, don't dawdle. Come straight home. We don't want to get her in trouble by making him wait."

Papa didn't see anything wrong with Agnes and me walking to the candy store and back. When he told Agnes's father about it he sounded so matter of fact that I guess the man couldn't say anything but yes. Mama came out and handed me two pennies and we started down the walk. I turned once to look behind but her brother was the only one watching us. His face looked so wistful that I knew he wanted to go, too. Maybe he'd never been downtown himself.

I had a little trouble getting Agnes to walk with me. She wanted to walk single-file, the way Indians do, but when I told her people would think we were strange she didn't argue.

As it was, some of them thought we were strange anyway. The Petersons were all sitting on their front porch, and when I spoke to them neither Ethel Marie or Helen May answered. They were too busy staring, and Ethel Marie's bug eyes were almost popping from her head.

Since it was a nice day, almost everyone was outside, although Mama and I were the only ones actually planting seeds in the front. Everybody stared, and everybody except the Petersons spoke.

Agnes didn't even notice the people. Her black eyes were shiny and she turned her head from side to side so she wouldn't miss anything.

"I didn't know whites had such fine houses," she said.

They weren't fine. There are a couple in Maple Glen that are sort of fancy, with turrets and lots of gingerbread trimming and a stained glass window or two, but they weren't on this street. I wondered what her own house looked like.

"Don't you ever get splinters on your feet?" I asked curiously. The board sidewalks are old, and in the summer I always walk on the grass because splinters can really dig in.

"Too many callouses. Splinters can't go through." She looked down at her bare feet and laughed, covering her mouth as she had before.

When we got to Main Street, her eyes got almost as big as Ethel Marie's. There must have been one store at least on the reservation, but we had three blocks of them, on both sides of the street. I was kept busy explaining about them, and Agnes wanted to stop and peer in every window but I knew we didn't have time.

She wasn't impressed with the courthouse, although it's very fine, built of gray stone with a cupola holding the clock, just with the stores and the things they had to sell.

Only the candy store was open on Sunday and when we got inside Agnes grew shy again. She wouldn't speak. She wouldn't even point when I told her she could spend her penny for anything she wanted. She whispered for me to pick, and finally I got us each a long black licorice whip, since it would take longest to eat.

"Now, we've really got to hurry home," I told her when we got outside. "Your father will be wanting to start back."

The reminder of her father was all it took. She did not stop to look in windows or stare at houses. We came home at a gallop, and as we turned in at the gate and saw them still sitting on the bench, her breath came out in a little gasp of relief.

They must have been ready to go because as soon as they saw us her father and brother got to their feet. Mama had gone back in the house, but Papa got up too and followed his callers down the walk. Their old wagon, drawn by two mangy horses, was waiting in the street.

The older Indian climbed onto the seat and his son after him. Agnes was still standing by the wagon. I don't know where she had held it, but now she brought out the long licorice whip. I had been chewing on mine, but hers was without a tooth mark. She measured it out and broke it into thirds. One piece she handed up to her father, another to her brother. Then, with the third dangling from her own mouth, she stepped on the wheel and hoisted herself into the back of the wagon.

"Good-bye, Marty," she called from her licorice-coated mouth. "I liked to see your town."

Chapter 6

MAMA WASN'T FEELING WELL the next morning, she was lying on the lounge in the front room when I came downstairs, and because of the clattering sounds in the kitchen, I remembered it was Mrs. Barndecker's day to clean.

Mama has what Aunt Gertrude calls "female trouble" and once a month she has to stay off her feet. I knew it was my fault because once I had heard Aunt Gertrude tell her that if she hadn't had me when she was so old it never would have happened. Mama said that wasn't so and even if it were true I was worth every bit of it. They didn't know I was listening, but I always felt guilty and took care to be very good when she had one of her spells.

I tiptoed into the front room and asked if I could do anything for her before I left.

"Not a thing, dear," said Mama. She smiled but I could see dark circles under her eyes so she hadn't slept very well. "I probably did a little too much yesterday. But I'll be all right when I rest. I told Mrs. Barndecker to keep your breakfast warm. You'd better run and eat or you'll be late for school."

"I'll hurry straight home afterwards," I promised. "So don't you do a thing. Just lie there and read your book."

Mama said she would and I went to the kitchen where Mrs. Barndecker was getting ready to clean the ashes from the stove. She hadn't bothered to keep my breakfast hot, but had let the fire go out and now she had newspapers spread all around the stove.

Any other day I would have squawked bloody murder, but I didn't want to upset Mama when she wasn't feeling well. Mrs. Barndecker must have been counting on that because she just kind of smirked while I ladled lukewarm mush into a bowl. I got even with her though. I didn't fill the cooking pot with water when it was empty. Instead I put it back on the stove where the mush would harden on the sides and she'd have to scour it out.

"Hear you been consorting with some Injun from the reservation," said Mrs. Barndecker when she saw I wasn't going to say anything about the cold mush. "Took her straight up Main Street on the Sabbath and even bought her candy."

"How'd you hear about that?" I stopped eating to stare at her. Mrs. Barndecker lived at the opposite end of town, near the mill. She couldn't possibly have seen us.

"Oh, I got my ways," she told me smugly. "Your ma and pa know about it?"

"Of course, they did. Mama even gave me the pennies to spend."

"Well!" said Mrs. Barndecker.

"Agnes is a nice girl," I told her indignantly. "She's every bit as good as you."

Mrs. Barndecker didn't answer. She just went on sweeping ashes.

I pushed away my bowl. The mush was horrible and I couldn't eat another mouthful. The only thing I wanted was to get away from her. I wished we had another cleaning woman, but it was hard to find somebody to do housework in Maple Glen.

I stopped in to see Mama for a minute before I left, and while I was talking there was a timid knock on the front door.

"It's probably Yuey Kim after the washing," guessed Mama. He picked it up every Monday morning. "Will you get it for him, Marty? It's in my room, all ready to go. I did it as soon as I got up."

Yuey Kim was one of the ugliest men I've ever seen, Chinese or white, but I liked him. His face was covered with pockmarks and his nose was pushed to one side as though it might have been broken and not straightened out. He wore white trousers with a loose white shirt, sort of like a middy blouse, hanging on the outside, a straw hat that came up to a peak like an Indian tepee and straw sandals. But he had a nice smile. Some people said he was scary because he shuffled along so glumly, but he always smiled at me.

"Hello, Yuey Kim," I said when I opened the door and saw him standing there. "I'll get the washing. My mama's sick today. Do you want to come in while you wait?"

"No, Missy." He smiled that wide, friendly smile that cracked his face like a ripe melon that's fallen to the ground. "You get wash. Yucy Kim wait here.

"Missus very sick?" he inquired anxiously when I came back struggling with the huge bundle tied up in a sheet. "Yuey Kim help maybe?"

"No, there's nothing you can do. She'll be all right after she rests." I watched in admiration as he swung the heavy bundle, which I could barely drag, over his shoulder. "But thank you."

"This week bring back wash Thursday, not Friday," he promised. "Missy be here maybe?"

"In the afternoon. When school is out."

"Yuey Kim come then," he said nodding. "Bring Missy lychee nuts?"

"That would be nice," I agreed. "I love lychee nuts."

Mr. Webster's grocery didn't carry them. I hadn't even known what they were until Yuey Kim had brought me a handful a few years ago. Now he always seemed to have a couple in one of the pockets of his shirt, and he presented them with one of his wide smiles whenever he returned our laundry. He hadn't expected to see me this morning or he would have been prepared.

I suppose I should have been warned by Mrs. Barndecker, but I wasn't. The minute I got to school I knew that the story of me taking Agnes to the candy store had made the rounds. People looked at me and laughed, sometimes it was out loud, sometimes it was just a sly smile. The trouble was I couldn't see anything to laugh at.

Fay Phipps was the first to speak of it openly.

"You didn't really, did you, Marty?" she whispered while I was hanging up my coat. "Really walk down the street with an Injun from the reservation and buy her candy?"

"Of course, I did. Her father had come to see Papa on business and brought her along. When she told me she'd never seen a real town, I thought she ought to. What would you have done?"

"I'd have shown her the way and let her go by herself," said Fay promptly. "You didn't have to walk with her. And was she really barefooted? It's only March and cold."

"She probably doesn't own any shoes. And anyway she said her feet were calloused. How'd you hear about it anyway?"

"Ethel Marie and Helen May. They're telling everybody," reported Fay reproachfully.

I was so mad I couldn't think of anything to say, but just then the bell rang so I didn't have to.

At recess, though, it started again. The minute I got out on the playground Freddy Taylor gave a war whoop, and before long all the boys were doing it too. Some of them looked a little bewildered, but as soon as they found out about Agnes they whooped even louder.

I marched straight over to where Ethel Marie was standing with some of her eighth-grade friends.

"I hear you're telling everybody I took an Indian girl downtown and bought her candy. What's so funny about that?"

"And you can't deny it," said Ethel Marie triumphantly. "Because I saw it with my own eyes. Everybody on our street did."

"I'm not denying it. She'd never seen a town before." I was so mad I could hear the shaking in my own voice. "She'd never been inside a real store, only an Indian trading post. Her father had come to see Papa on business, and he wouldn't even drive down Main Street on the way back."

"At least he knows his place," said Helen May.

"She didn't have shoes!" Ethel Marie explained to the others. "And she looked dirty. And there they were, the two of them, walking along on a Sunday afternoon gawking at everybody."

"She was too scared to go by herself. And it didn't hurt me," I insisted.

"You're strange anyway," said Ethel Marie. She turned to the others. "Would you believe it? Marty picks up dead birds with her bare hands. And she's got a pet cemetery in her yard where she buries dead animals. She even puts flowers on their graves. And in the summer her mother lets her wear overalls just like a boy. But this is the worst. The absolute worst. All I can say is, 'Birds of a feather flock together!'"

"I don't think it was so bad of Marty to show that Indian

girl our town," said Marian Tilson. "I think it was nice. It showed a good Christian spirit."

I couldn't believe my ears. Marian Tilson was one of the leaders in the eighth grade. Everybody sort of looked up to her, and she was the last person I ever expected to stand up for me. Ethel Marie turned fire engine red and all the others looked from her to Marian with their mouths open. I could almost see them trying to decide whose side they were going to be on.

"Of course, I wouldn't touch a dead bird," continued Marian loftily. "Only with a stick. And Marty is a little too old to have a pet cemetery. But as for the Indian girl, I think she did just right."

"But the boy's overalls," persisted Ethel Marie desperately.

"I wouldn't wear them myself," admitted Marian. "But I can see how they'd be useful if you were picking something like hops or blackberries that scratched your legs."

"They are," affirmed Fay Phipps. I hadn't noticed, but she'd followed and was standing just behind me. "I wish my grandma would buy me some, but she's too old-fashioned. My legs are a mess after I've been picking berries."

Everybody began agreeing that leg coverings would be useful at such times and talking about the bad scratches they had suffered in the past. In the discussion they seemed to forget about me, so Fay and I left.

"I never thought Marian Tilson would stick up for me," I said.

"Oh, she'd stick up for anybody that Ethel Marie didn't like," replied Fay cheerfully. "Didn't you know they hate each other?"

A minute before I'd been feeling pretty good, but now I felt all let down again. It wasn't so comforting to know that Marian had only taken my side because Ethel Marie was against me.

But they were just one group. All day people kept staring at me and sort of tittering or giving war whoops and I was glad when school was over. I lit out for home by the back streets as fast as I could go.

I'd come home at noon for lunch but Mama had been asleep, so I didn't wake her. I ate the sandwich and soup that Mrs. Barndecker had fixed for me and then waited till the very last minute to go back. I hadn't planned to tell Mama about my day until she was feeling better, but she already knew. When I got home the second time, Aunt Gertrude was there before me.

"I don't know what you could have been thinking of, Bea," she was saying as I walked in. "When Reva Peterson called me I was simply flabbergasted. For once I didn't know what to say."

"That's hard for me to believe, Gertrude," said Mama dryly. "But I'm sure you thought of something."

"Just that I would talk to you, of course," Aunt Gertrude told her huffily. "And that I was sure you didn't know what Marty had done."

Aunt Gertrude is a big woman, with dark hair like Mama's, but without her dimples. She never goes anywhere without her corset, so she isn't wobbly fat, and she's very particular about her clothes. She likes pale blue with little printed figures on it, and her hats are always set precisely on her head. She wouldn't dream of going downtown without a hat and gloves, even if she's just grocery shopping. She always works on some committee or the other and she has a lot of friends. People think a lot of Gertrude Potter in Maple Glen. I do too, sometimes, because she can be very nice when she wants to, but I'm glad she isn't my mother.

"Oh, but I did know," said Mama quickly. "I thought it

was nice of Marty to show the girl our town. She'd never seen one, you know."

"But parading her down the street that way," wailed Aunt Gertrude. "Reva Peterson said she was dirty and ragged. Why she wasn't even wearing shoes!"

"When the weather's hot, I let Marty go barefoot," Mama reminded her.

"There's absolutely no sense in talking to you, Bea," declared Aunt Gertrude angrily. "You never did care what people said about you. But you're my sister. Marty's my niece. What you do reflects on the rest of the family and you should think of us. Think of Sam's position, if nothing else. How does it look for the daughter of the county judge to be seen with a savage? And since you brought it up yourself, to let her go barefoot in the summer is scandalous. All the other girls wear shoes and stockings."

"Sam agrees with me. He's very particular about Marty's feet. Going barefoot in the summer is good for them. As for taking that Indian girl downtown yesterday, he approved of that, too."

"I give up," said Aunt Gertrude, hoisting herself to her feet. "As for the Indian, I'll tell everybody that when I saw you today you had taken to your bed with one of your spells. And that yesterday it was probably coming on and you didn't know what you were doing when you permitted such a thing. Have you heard from Andy?" She changed the subject abruptly.

"No. He doesn't write to us." Mama stopped looking angry and grew concerned. "Haven't you heard lately?"

"Not for several weeks. Then he was in the trenches. He didn't tell us where. Maybe they wouldn't let him. He asked if we'd send him socks. Apparently the army issue's not enough."

"I'll start knitting a pair right away," promised Mama. "And I wouldn't worry. Andy was never much of a letter writer, was he?"

"No, he wasn't," agreed Aunt Gertrude. "And no news is good news. Horace says the overseas mail usually arrives in a batch, and as postmaster he ought to know. Maybe we'll hear today."

"I hope so," said Mama quickly.

"And as you say, he never was a letter writer," agreed Aunt Gertrude, brightening up a little. "Otherwise he's a fine boy. Almost a perfect son except for that one failing. He never was one to write letters. Well, I'll just run along, and on the way I'll drop in a minute and tell Reva Peterson how sick you are. That will explain a lot."

After she had gone. Mama and I looked at each other, and I could tell by her face how sorry she was.

"Did you take a lot of abuse today, Marty?" she asked finally.

"A little." I didn't want her to know how bad it had been.

"Are you sorry you took the girl downtown and bought her candy?"

I had to think that over awhile.

"No," I decided finally. "It meant a lot to her, and as for the kids at school, they'll forget it after a while."

Mama winced at the word "kids" but that time she didn't correct me.

"Sometimes, when something like this happens, I wish we lived in a city," she said. "Maybe people there would have more to think about and they wouldn't be so concerned with petty things. But it probably wouldn't help. There are bigots everyplace. I hope you can learn to rise above them."

Chapter 7

IT TOOK ABOUT A WEEK for the kids at school to forget about Agnes. In the meantime I went about pretending I didn't care, which is the best way to handle things like that, and it worked. But I didn't forget how Fay had stood by me or how Marian Tilson stuck up for me even if it was because of Ethel Marie. And I didn't forget that everybody thought I was too old for a pet cemetery.

I told Mama about that finally, and we agreed it would be a good idea to take away the stone markers on the graves and plant a flower bed over the top. It would be like a memorial garden. She said I could start a new cemetery if I wanted, but it had better be someplace in the barnyard where no one could see it from the street.

I hoped I wouldn't have to use it, but one morning we got up and Tiger was dead. Papa said it looked to him like poison. Maybe someone had put it out for a rat and Tiger had caught the rat that ate it. He told me to pick out a place and he would bury Tiger while I was at Sunday school. I wanted to be there, but he said it was better for me not to see. I guess poor old Tiger didn't look very pretty.

As soon as I got home, I changed my clothes and he took me out to the barnyard. He'd dug Tiger's grave not far from the millrace and next to the Hutchinsons' wall, just as the first pet cemetery had been. It was a long way from the street and protected by some thimbleberry bushes. Even Mrs. Hershy couldn't see it from her kitchen window.

When I stood looking down at the freshly dug mound I kept thinking about Tiger and I felt a tear running down my cheek. Papa put his arm around me.

"He was a good cat, honey," he reminded me. "And he had a good life, all nine of them."

"Cats don't have nine lives, Papa," I told him reproachfully. "Or those little kittens wouldn't have died."

"Maybe you're right," he agreed seriously. "I never thought of that. Now why don't you pick some flowers for Tiger? It will look a lot better when you fix it up a little."

There were plenty of flowers in bloom by now, and I even got some jelly jars so they would have water and last longer. I was glad Papa hadn't come back with me while I decorated the grave, because I wanted to be alone.

But I wasn't alone. No sooner had I finished singing the hymn when there it was—three knocks from the Hutchinsons' side of the wall. I was so mad I could hardly see straight.

"Miss Rebecca, this is private!" I shouted. "I'm just burying my cat and I don't want you here. Go back to your house."

Instead of doing as I said there were two knocks. I stood there, shaking with anger, and pretty soon there were two more. It occurred to me then that she was telling me "no." It was our code. One knock for yes. Two knocks for no.

I had just decided to ignore her entirely when I heard a tiny little voice coming through the boards.

"I'm sorry about your cat."

I had never heard Miss Rebecca speak. I suppose she knew

how or she couldn't ask for things at Webster's Grocery Store, but somehow the voice didn't sound the way I thought she would. It wasn't a woman's voice. It was a child's.

"Are you Miss Rebecca?" I asked, stepping closer to the fence and wishing there was even a tiny crack between the boards.

I wasn't surprised at the two knocks, since I'd seen Mrs. Hutchinson and Miss Rebecca going in the church door when I left Sunday school. Miss Rebecca couldn't keep on forever making excuses to leave, and besides there was that little voice, which couldn't come from a grownup.

"Who are you then?" I asked, but there was nothing but silence in return.

"Listen," I said as patiently as I could, "if I promise not to tell a soul about you, will you talk to me? It's silly to keep knocking on the wall the way you do."

There was a long pause and then a single knock, yes.

"All right," I told her. "I swear. Cross my heart and hope to die, stick a finger in my eye. I won't tell a single living soul about you. Not even Papa or Mama. It will be just our secret. Now, who are you?"

"Sinette," quavered the little voice finally.

"Sinette?" I wasn't sure I had heard correctly. It was a name I'd never heard before. "Did you say Sinette?"

"Yes." The voice was so low I could hardly hear it.

"That's a very unusual name," I told her, trying to think of something nice to say about it.

"I hate it." This time the voice was louder, angry.

"Then why don't you take a nickname? My name's really Martha, but nobody ever calls me that. When I was just learning to talk, I couldn't say it very well. I called myself Marty, and it just stuck with me. Nobody ever calls me

Martha—except maybe new teachers on the first day of school and my grandma. I'm named for her. That's what you must do. Pick a nickname."

"Mrs. Hutchinson wouldn't let me."

"What's she got to say about it?" But I knew the answer even before I asked. Mrs. Hutchinson, that old bat, was probably keeping the poor girl prisoner inside the wall. Just wait till I told Papa about it! He'd have her out in no time. And then I remembered. I couldn't tell Papa. I'd sworn not to tell anyone.

"She named me," explained the girl. "Sinette means 'little sin,' and whenever we hear it Rebecca and I remember that's what I am. A sin."

"Is Rebecca your mother?"

"Yes. Only I don't call her that."

"Then Mrs. Hutchinson must be your grandmother!"

"Yes, but I don't call her that, either. I don't call her anything."

"How old are you, S—?" I caught myself just in time. We'd think up a new name, one that she liked. How horrible to go through life being called "Little Sin."

"I'm ten."

"Have you always lived there in that house, with the wall around it?"

"Yes. But from the attic window I can see into your yard. That's how I knew about you. I watch you all the time."

It gave me a funny feeling to know that for ten years somebody had been watching everything I did when I was in our yard.

"Won't they let you come out at all?"

"No. I have to stay here. That's so no one will know about me," she explained.

"They're keeping you a prisoner against your will," I told her angrily. "And that's against the law. My papa's a lawyer. If you'll just let me tell him—"

"No," she interrupted quickly. "You mustn't. You promised. I wouldn't have told you at all if I'd thought you wouldn't keep your word."

"Oh, I won't tell. I promised. And I won't break my promise." After I knew her a little better, I told myself, I'd get her to release me from that promise. Papa would have her out of there in two shakes of a lamb's tail. In the meantime, the thing to do was to get her to trust me.

"What would you like me to call you?" I asked. "I'm certainly not going to call you Sinette. Not when you don't like it."

"I don't know," she answered helplessly.

"Oh, there are lots of names," I assured her quickly. "Let's see. There's Sarah—no, that's too plain. Sylvia is nice. Patty—that's short for Patricia. Lloyd—that's in a book about *The Little Colonel.* I've always liked it even if it is generally a boy's name. Elizabeth or Betty, Barbara—do you like any of those?"

"Sometimes, when Mrs. Hutchinson has gone to the hardware store, Rebecca calls me Antoinette," she told me hesitantly. "That's what she wanted to name me, only Mrs. Hutchinson wouldn't let her."

"Antoinette!" I was a little surprised that Miss Rebecca would have picked out a name like that. She was so mousy herself that I would have expected her to choose something more common. "That's beautiful. It was the name of a queen."

"I know. Only she got killed. I read about her in a book."

"You can read and write?"

"Rebecca teaches me. I read a lot, only we don't have many books. Most of them are sermons and things. Mrs. Hutchinson doesn't spend money on books."

"I have a lot of them. I could loan you—"

"No," she objected quickly. "Somebody might see one. Then they'd know I'd been talking to you. And I'm not supposed to do that."

She was pretty smart to think of such a thing. I would have taken a chance. Hidden the book and only brought it out when it was safe, like late at night.

"How about your father?" I asked. "Does he know they keep you shut up like this?"

"I don't have a father. I never had one."

"But you have to have had."

"No," she insisted. "I don't. I'd better go to the house now. Rebecca and Mrs. Hutchinson should be coming back soon."

"Wait," I called desperately. "Wait, Antoinette. When can I talk to you again?"

"Sunday," she told me. "It's the only time that's really safe. They'll both be at church."

"I'll be here," I promised. "Bye, Antoinette. Talk to you next week."

There was no answer, so I knew she'd run to her house, fearful lest church might be over early.

I went back inside, trying to fit what Antoinette had told me with Mrs. Hershy's gossip. She must have been brought here when she was a baby, but how Mrs. Hutchinson and Miss Rebecca could have kept the secret all those years I couldn't imagine. Probably she was born during that year Miss Rebecca was supposed to be visiting relatives in Seattle. But now that I thought of it, I wondered if there really were any relatives in Seattle. Certainly they had never visited in Maple Glen or Mrs. Hershy would have known about them.

Papa was reading the Sunday paper in the dining room. He was sitting in the Morris chair with his feet propped up on the mantel, the way he always did.

"All finished, honey?" He stopped reading to look at me above the top of his reading glasses.

For a minute I couldn't think what he meant. Then I remembered Tiger.

"All finished," I told him. "The grave looks very nice. I found a lot of flowers."

"Good. Tomorrow, if you want to, we'll see if we can't find you a new kitten."

"Not now, Papa. I think we should wait awhile."

"All right. But when you're ready, we won't have any trouble. This is the time for spring kittens. I have a lot of friends who have barn cats. I'll drive you around and you can take your pick."

"There'll never be another Tiger."

"Of course not. Each cat is an individual. They're just like people. But you can remember Tiger for what he was and love a new kitten for different reasons."

"If I could find a cat exactly like Tiger it wouldn't be so bad," I admitted. "But he didn't have any kittens."

"Don't be so sure," insisted Papa. "Tiger was a big, healthy tom. He probably fathered kittens for miles around. Don't you remember how sometimes he was missing a couple of days? Then he'd come home, a little battered, but he got here."

"You mean he just left the kittens and forgot about them?"

"It's the nature of cats," Papa told me. "And of dogs and horses and lots of animals."

My mind turned to Antoinette, who didn't have a father, or one she ever knew. "But not people?"

"Sometimes even people. Not very nice people, of course, but it happens."

Antoinette said she had never had a father and I wondered if that could have happened to her. I didn't stop to think about it much then though because there was something else I needed to know.

"Papa, is it legal to keep a person shut up in a place for years and never let him go outside or talk to anyone else?"

"Only if he's been sentenced by the court to some place like the penitentiary." He looked a little surprised. "Why?"

"I just wondered," I said hastily and went up to my room.

During dinner Papa and Mama talked about the war. Things weren't going too well. England and France were both exhausted from all the fighting they had done before we got into it. And the fresh American troops, for whom everybody had such hopes, had been driven back from some battle or the other. I didn't understand it too much and I didn't try too hard because it was all so far away.

"We're going to step up the draft," said Papa. "It will include married men whose wives are able to support themselves now."

"Are there many of them?" asked Mama.

"More than you'd think," he answered her. "Some of these farm women can plow as straight a furrow as their husbands. We're all pioneer stock, you know."

"There were three more gold stars reported at church this morning," said Mama sadly. "Kermit Reed, Woodrow Worley and Dan Sanders. Dan was a special friend of Andy's. All fine young men, and all giving their lives for their country. Just from this little town. There's something wrong with the world, Sam."

"What about Ralph Hershy?" I asked.

"I'm afraid he's had it," said Papa, grinning a little. "He can't plead dependent parents any longer, not with what Bill Hershey has in the bank. We didn't know about his safety deposit box before, but Ed Cox couldn't stand it any longer. He let it out."

Poor Mrs. Hershy, I thought. I was sorry for her but not for Ralph. Anybody who shot cats could shoot Huns.

Apparently they didn't lose any time getting to Ralph, because when I came home from school the next day there was a flag with a blue star hanging in the window. Mrs. Hershy must have been watching for me, because when I stopped to stare she threw open the door and beckoned to me.

"I suppose you heard, Marty," she said, beaming. "My Ralphie's off to fight the Germans. Or he will be in a day or two. Ralphie's such a fine young man. Sickly as he is, he wanted to do his part."

"Was he drafted?" I asked cautiously.

"Gracious no," she assured me promptly. "First thing this morning he went down and enlisted. The rumor's out they're going to start taking married men and Ralphie says that means they're scraping the barrel. I knew it would happen sometime. I've had this service flag laid away in the drawer for months. I don't know how me and William will manage without him, but we'll make out. And nobody can ever call Ralphie a slacker again, now can they?"

"No, Mrs. Hershy," I said. "They certainly can't."

Chapter 8

THERE WERE A LOT OF CHANGES in those next weeks in Maple Glen. Every man who wasn't too old or too young, who had what Papa called a non-essential job, was drafted into the army. The clerks in the stores had always been men, but now their wives took their places behind the counters. Uncle Horace Potter, who was as old as Papa, was the only man left in the post office, and ladies sorted mail and put it in the boxes. There were a lot more women in the courthouse, too, in places like the recorders' office, and there wasn't a man working in either of our two cafes; a woman did the cooking and older girls waited on tables.

"More manpower," said Papa firmly. "That's what the army wants, that's what we'll give them."

Mama worked two days a week at the Red Cross now instead of one, and Aunt Gertrude was there every day with a white cloth draped over her head. Besides our rolls of tinfoil, children were told to collect a lot of other things: scraps of copper, brass, iron and zinc, burlap gunnysacks, collapsible paste or paint tubes and magazines and newspapers folded and tied with string. I couldn't imagine what they wanted with all this junk, but collecting it was our part in the war effort.

"It has its uses," said Aunt Gertrude. I'd asked her what they were going to do with it because, as head of our local Red Cross, I thought she'd be most likely to know. "Germany's doing it too. Why I hear that they've required every German to remove the metal lid of beer steins to melt down into bullets. It should make a lot of them. I understand the Germans drink a lot of beer. Ugh!"

We had Prohibition[1] now and Jake's Saloon was closed up tighter than a rusty box.

The saddest thing was that the candy store went out of business. They couldn't get sugar. Now sugar was only sold in two and five pound bags, and you could only buy so much. So at home all our desserts were made with honey. One of Papa's clients always paid his bill with that, so we had plenty. But it tasted kind of funny in some things.

I could hardly wait for Sunday so I could visit with Antoinette again. I'd talked with her once since that first time, but I hadn't found out anything new. In fact, I'd done most of the talking. Once she started you couldn't shut her up. She was just full of questions about what it was like outside the walls and about my school and what I did. By the time I got through answering everything, she had to go back to her house so she'd be there when Mrs. Hutchinson and Miss Rebecca got home from church. There wasn't time for me to ask anything.

This week was going to be different. This time I'd ask the questions. But there were still three more days to go.

I liked our evenings best. Unless it was lodge night for one of my parents, or Saturday, when we generally went to the moving picture show, we read aloud. We'd sit around the fireplace, me in the middle, Papa in his Morris chair on one side, Mama in her rocker on the other, and take turns. We

1. Prohibition begin in 1916 in Oregon.

read the classics, because Mama said we couldn't depend on the schools to give them to me. Dickens and Scott and Dumas—my, how I loved *The Three Musketeers* and *Twenty Years After* and *The Man in the Iron Mask*—and Poe and Stevenson, things like that. My parents were good readers and they made things come alive. The sentences were long and some of the words were hard, but whoever was reading always stopped and explained. It was very interesting.

Tonight Mama brought out a new book.

"It's *The Scarlet Letter* by Nathaniel Hawthorne," she told us. "High time we got into the American authors."

"We've already read Poe and Stevenson." Papa raised his white bushy eyebrows. "Don't you think *The Scarlet Letter* is a little old for Marty?"

"No, I don't," said Mama positively. "That's the way things were in that period of history, and besides I've very carefully explained the facts of life to her."

"It's about an adulteress," Papa told me. "Do you know what adultery is, Marty?"

"Of course," I told him promptly. "It's one of the Ten Commandments. 'Thou shalt not commit adultery.' It's like Tiger going off to start kittens without being married."

"Of course, what happened to Hester Prynne a hundred years ago could never happen now," Mama said earnestly. "Adultery is still a disgrace, but people don't sew the letter A on the dresses of those who are guilty of it and make them stand in the pillory. We're too civilized for that."

"What do we do?" I demanded.

"Well, I guess most people try to hide it." It was the first time I'd ever seen Mama embarrassed. "Maybe they put the baby out for adoption. But it's still a disgrace, of course."

"Like Edna Pope's mother?" Even as I asked I felt guilty remembering that I hadn't called on her as she had asked.

Mama frowned but Papa answered for both of them.

"Like Edna Pope's mother," he agreed.

"What about the baby? Do the grandparents always take it?"

"Not always. Sometimes it's adopted by strangers who want a child. If they don't tell it, it will never know they weren't its real parents."

"But what if nobody wants it?" I demanded.

"It's sent to an orphanage. Sometimes the mother leaves the baby in a church or even an ash can and sneaks away. She hopes to avoid scandal for herself."

"That's enough, Sam," said Mama reprovingly. She opened the book and began to read aloud. One thing about Mama and Papa, they always skipped the long introductions and got right down to the story. They said I could read the introductions, which were often boring, when I was older.

I didn't listen too carefully to the first part, but when it was my turn to read I had to concentrate. I was sure that the man in the crowd watching poor Hester Prynne on the pillory was the father of the baby. And when he put his finger on his lips, which meant he wanted her to keep quiet about him, I was sure. Horrible man. How could anyone act like that? The book got more interesting as it went along.

When the mantle clock chimed nine, we closed the book and went to bed. By that time not only our voices but our eyes were tired. But even so I couldn't go to sleep for a long time. Instead of Hester Prynne, I kept thinking about Antoinette and wondering what I could do to help her. I couldn't think of anything at all.

When Yuey Kim returned our laundry that week he also brought gifts. That was nothing new. He was always bringing us presents. But this time he brought more than usual. There was a little stone jar, laced with raffia, and filled with candied ginger for Mama. And besides the usual lychee nuts, he brought me a little carved figure of a Chinese man with a very fat stomach.

"This Chinese good luck god," he told me. "Missy rub his stomach every morning, have good luck all day."

"Oh, Yuey Kim," said Mama helplessly. "You shouldn't have done this. You're always bringing us things, and this time I haven't a thing for you. That idol looks awfully old. It must be valuable."

"Yuey Kim bring him from China," he admitted. "Always he bring good luck. Just rub his tummy. Want Missy to have him. Bring her good luck too. Yuey Kim buy a new one tomorrow in Chinatown."

He smiled his wide broken-faced smile, and we knew he hadn't expected gifts in return.

"Yuey Kim late next week picking up wash," he told Mama. "Go to Portland tomorrow. Get wash Tuesday."

"That's fine," she told him. "You have a good time. You've earned it. It must be lonely around here, being the only Chinese. But in Portland's Chinatown you probably have a lot of friends."

"I go for business also," he admitted. "Yuey Kim be here Tuesday."

"Now what can I do?" asked Mama as she closed the door. "I'll bake him something Tuesday, though I never know if he likes the things I bake or not. That's a valuable idol, Marty."

She took it from my hands and rubbed her fingers over it lightly.

"It looks very old, not something brought in for tourists. Take good care of it."

I promised I would and carried it up to my room. From my window I could see the third floor attic windows of the

Hutchinson house next door. From one of them Antoinette had watched me in our yard, and I wondered if she'd been there today. If she had been, she was gone now.

Sunday finally came and I raced home from Sunday school as fast as I could.

"I'm going to take some flowers to Tiger," I told Papa, who was reading his Sunday papers. I looked at the stack beside him and decided it would take him quite a while to get through them.

"Never was a cat so dearly loved or remembered," said Papa. "Don't forget to tell me when you're ready for his successor. Maybe we could find a yellow one this time. You've never had a yellow kitten."

"Maybe," I agreed and dashed upstairs to change my clothes. I put two sticks of Black Jack gum in the pocket of my sweater. I'd had them a long time because they'd been pushed back into a bureau drawer and I'd forgotten about them. But Antoinette wouldn't know the difference.

The last time we'd talked I'd had a piece of gum in my mouth and kept popping it the way you do. She asked me about the funny noise and when I told her it was chewing gum, she wanted to know all about it. She'd never had a stick of gum. There probably were a lot of ordinary things, the kind we took for granted, she'd never had. But we'd start with the gum.

I snapped off a few daffodils for Tiger as I went by, just in case Papa saw the grave and wondered what I'd been doing, then I went to the barnyard. Antoinette must have heard me coming because as soon as I got there she began rapping on the wall.

"You can just stop that," I told her firmly. "I'm all alone. And I brought you a stick of gum."

"Chewing gum? The kind you told me about last week?"

She actually squeaked in her excitement.

"Yes. It's a little stale because I've had it awhile, so you'll have to chew hard at first to get it started. Now remember, you're not supposed to swallow it. When you're tired of chewing, spit it out. Where nobody will step on it, either."

"But how are you going to get it to me?" she asked anxiously. "Can you throw it over the wall?"

"I don't think so. It's too light. But I thought if I found a shingle, a little one, I could put the gum on top and float it through one of the holes in the wall down the millrace. You'll have to catch it as it goes by. Can you do that?"

"Oh, yes." Then she seemed to hesitate. "Marty—"

"Yes." I was looking around for a shingle the right size to go through the hole.

"Before you give me any presents there's something I have to tell you. It's about me," she continued. "And when you know you may not want to talk to me through the wall or give me chewing gum."

"What's the matter with you? Do you have leprosy?" We'd been talking about lepers in Sunday school just that morning, which made them pop into my mind.

"No. It's about my father."

"Oh. Well, you had to have one, whether you knew him or not," I told her practically.

"I know. But my m— Rebecca wasn't married to him. That's why Mrs. Hutchinson calls me Sinette. It's a great disgrace. We have to spend the rest of our lives making up for it."

In the back of my mind, I'd known this all the time, but having her come out with it like that almost took my wind away. Of course, in history all the kings of Europe had illegitimate children. They were called a word beginning with *B*, which Mama said I mustn't say. The king usually gave them titles and nobody thought anything about it. But that was Europe. This was Maple Glen and I didn't think Maple Glen would be very nice to someone who was a word beginning with *B*. They had been mean enough about Edna Pope.

"It's not your fault," I told her, realizing the silence was getting a little long. "It doesn't matter to me a whiffle. You're not to blame for what happened. I never did believe that stuff in the Bible about the sins of the father being visited on his generations."

"Didn't you?" She gasped. "Mrs. Hutchinson reads us that part every night. She says the Bible is law."

"I bet you she didn't read you the part about 'He who is without sin cast the first stone,' though," I pointed out. It's funny how many of the things you hear in Sunday school can rub off on you, and I was a little proud when that came back to me. Mama and Papa and I didn't talk about the Bible much. They just wanted me to be good and to be nice to everybody. I try to be, except for Ethel Marie Peterson. No one could be nice to her.

"No—no, she didn't," quavered Antoinette.

"Well, it's there," I told her flatly. "It's the law, too. You've got absolutely nothing to do with who your parents are. So of course I'm your friend. Now, I found a piece of shingle and you go down to the millrace. I'll put the gum on top and send it through. And don't eat the paper," I added hastily. "Pull it off and throw it back in. The current will carry it away."

The shingle was just the right size to go through the hole. I laid the stick of Black Jack on top and pushed it through. The next minute I heard a squeak which changed to a wail.

"It got away! I tried to catch it, but it floated out and I couldn't catch it and now it's gone. Oh, Marty, now I'll never know what chewing gum tastes like!"

I was so disgusted that for a minute I didn't know what to

say. Anybody else would have sense enough to wade in and catch the shingle before the current took it. But Antoinette wasn't anybody. She'd probably never been allowed to fish for crawdaddies or even get her feet wet in the millrace.

I still had one stick of Black Jack left that I was saving for myself so I decided to be noble. I'd give it to her. But I certainly wasn't going to send it through the hole and let the millrace get it.

"I've got another," I told her. "And I'll tell you what I'm going to do. There's a tall ladder in the barn. I'll bring it over here and prop it up against the wall and drop the gum down to you."

At the same time, I told myself craftily, I could get a peek at this girl on the other side who was nothing but a voice. I was surprised at myself for not having thought of it before.

The ladder was very heavy. It took me a long time to drag it through the still-muddy barnyard. The chickens followed me, peering into the ruts with their shiny black eyes, hoping I'd unearthed a worm or two as I went. It took even longer to prop it up against the wall, but I was pleased the ladder was tall enough. Papa had used it for the barn roof, and it extended two or three feet above the top of the board wall.

I propped it at a slant in the soft dirt and began climbing gingerly. It seemed an awfully long way to the ground. On the other side I could hear Antoinette telling me to be careful, but I was too busy to answer. Even though the ends of the ladder were sunk into the soft earth it still teetered a little and got worse the higher I got.

At last I reached the top and peered over the boards, but I didn't see anything because Papa's voice was roaring at me in a way it never had before.

"Martha Morgan Burnham! Climb down from that ladder at once. At once, do you hear? And be careful!"

I had just time to drop the stick of gum over the top board before I had to start back down. It wasn't as scary going down as it had been climbing up because I knew Papa was holding the ladder.

"Now, young lady, just what is the meaning of this?" He was wearing his judge's face that I'd never expected to have turned on me.

"I—I don't know," I quavered. "It just seemed like a good idea. I've always wanted to see the Hutchinson's back yard."

"If Mrs. Hutchinson wanted you to see it, she would have asked you in," he said. "She put up the wall to keep people out. What you did was invasion of privacy, and that's a criminal offense."

"Yes, sir."

I wanted to tell him about Antoinette and how she'd never had chewing gum, but I couldn't. I'd promised I wouldn't.

"Now we'll put the ladder away, and don't you ever do such a thing again. Do you hear me?"

"Yes, sir. I promise." It would have been easier if he'd spanked me and got it over. But Papa never spanked me. That was always Mama's job, and even she had not done it many times, and not since I was a little girl. It was always enough when they looked at me the way Papa was looking now, as though I were a stranger and he wished I weren't his child.

Papa took one end of the ladder while I struggled with the other. He let me do it, too, although I've seen him carry it by himself many times. After we put the ladder away, he started back to the house and I tagged along behind wishing he would say something. Anything. But he didn't, not till we got inside when he told me curtly to go clean myself up. I was filthy.

When I got downstairs Mama was back from church and by the reproachful way she looked at me, I knew Papa had told her what I'd done. Neither one of them mentioned it again; and all through dinner they kept talking to each other about the war. I wished they'd say something to me except, "Please pass the butter," but they didn't. It was awful to have parents like that. In some ways it would have been better if they'd beaten me.

It wasn't until I got to bed that I thought about Antoinette and the stick of gum I'd tossed over the wall. I hoped she'd liked it even if it was awfully hard and stale.

Chapter 9

ON TUESDAY WE EXPECTED Yuey Kim to come for the laundry. Me, especially. Although he'd given me a present before he left, he always brought a little extra one from Chinatown. Sometimes it was a doll's paper parasol. Once it had been a straw thing that was called a finger trap. When you put a finger of each hand into a hole in two little cylinders and pulled, your fingers were caught. Another time it had been a tiny wooden boat that I could sail on the millrace. I always put a long string on that because I didn't want it to go floating through one of the holes in the Hutchinsons' wall.

But Tuesday came and went and Yuey Kim didn't appear. The same was true of Wednesday, and by Thursday Mama was getting a little irritated.

"It's just not like him," she told the ladies of the Red Cross, where they were sitting at a table rolling bandages. "He's always been so punctual."

I'd stopped in after school to check on her. It was one of her bad days and I was worried. But she said she'd be sitting down anyway and insisted on being there.

"He's an Oriental. You can't trust any of them," said Mrs. Edwards positively. "Besides he probably cheats you out of house and home. A sock here, a pillowcase there. It all counts up."

"You know the Yellow Peril. We've been warned about it enough," Mrs. Dawes reminded her darkly.

"Yuey Kim's not like that at all," Mama protested indignantly. "He's the soul of honesty, and he does such a nice job."

"I never was in favor of you using Chinese labor anyway, Bea," Aunt Gertrude reminded her. "I do all my own laundry, but if you want to waste your money on it, that's your business."

"There's a new steam laundry opening up. You can't say Maple Glen's not progressive," said Mrs. Edwards. "Run by a family named Brown. They've got one son named Henry that's in my Elmer's class at school. He's adopted though. Family makes no bones about it. I wouldn't be surprised if he wasn't illegitimate. I told Elmer to go slow on making friends with him."

All the ladies clucked like a flock of hens in a barnyard after one of them had found a worm.

"I'll wait a few more days for Yuey Kim," said Mama changing, the subject. "He may be back this weekend."

But he wasn't back by the weekend either, and then Papa found out why. It was so terrible that at first I couldn't believe it. My friend Yuey Kim, who always brought me lychee nuts and little presents, was dead. He had belonged to a Chinese club, called a tong, in Chinatown, and he was a hatchet man. That meant that when the Tong had trouble with another tong, they each sent for their hatchet men and the two of them fought it out. The only thing was they didn't use hatchets, they used pistols and this time the other hatchet man shot first. Aunt Gertrude said there was no telling how many men Yuey Kim had killed before it happened to him. But I didn't care.

I lay on my bed and cried and cried. Poor Yuey Kim. He'd had to hide out in a place like Maple Glen where he didn't have any friends. He was only sent for when there was trouble. No, that wasn't true. He had friends. Us. We'd liked him and he'd liked us. I got the little fat god of luck from the dresser and rubbed the smooth, polished stone again and again. Maybe if Yuey Kim hadn't given him to me, he'd still be alive. Maybe he hadn't had time to buy a new one, or if he had, the second hadn't been as powerful.

Mama came to get me after a while. She sat on the bed and smoothed my hair.

"Poor Marty," she said. "Life can be so hard. And it's too bad to learn it young."

"What'll happen to him, Mama?" I asked. "Can we bring him back here for the funeral?"

"He wouldn't want that. The tong will send him back to China. It's where Chinese want to be buried. In their own country."

"If he hadn't given me this—" I held out the fat, smiling idol.

"You know, I think he knew his time had come," said Mama thoughtfully. "He wasn't a young man. All those years, when we thought he was just a laundry man, he'd been making trips to Portland to carry out those jobs for his tong. No, I think he wanted you to have it, Marty, to remember him by. Take good care of it."

"Oh, I will," I promised. "I always will. But I'll miss him."

"We all will," she said a little grimly. "Especially when the steam laundry rips buttons from our shirts and makes tears in sheets."

I told Antoinette about Yuey Kim the next time we talked, and she was very sympathetic, not like the kids at school who either laughed and said he'd got what was coming to him or were horrified that a killer had been living in Maple Glen all these years. I decided Antoinette was my best friend, even though she was two years younger than me and I never saw her. The mud was drying out in the barnyard, so every Sunday during church I'd take a book out there and sit on the ground next to Tiger's grave and we'd talk.

If Papa came out there he'd just shake his head and say, "We ought to get you another kitten, Marty. Grieving over Tiger won't bring him back."

Then he'd go away and Antoinette and I would talk some more. Once in a while we could talk on the days when Mrs. Hutchinson went to her hardware store, but I never knew when Antoinette could be there. Miss Rebecca liked to spend that time with her daughter, so Antoinette could hardly ever come. I wondered if Miss Rebecca loved her.

I did most of the talking because nothing new ever happened to Antoinette. But that was all right. I liked to talk and she wanted to know every little thing I did.

One Sunday I was sitting there talking when Papa appeared. In his hands he held what looked like a fur ball.

"You were so long making up your mind about a new kitten, I just got you one," he said, holding out the ball. "Old Mrs. Wheeler had a litter of them when she called me out to make her will. She was delighted to get rid of one of them. This was the biggest and the feistiest of the bunch."

I took the fur ball from Papa's hands and it spit at me. It was yellow and its eyes were still baby blue, but it was the bravest, cutest kitten I had ever seen. It had a pretty face, like a flower, and pink ears when the sun shone through them and only part of a tail.

"It's half Manx," explained Papa, pointing to the tail. "The hind legs are a trifle long, too, like a rabbit's; which means that he'll be a jumper. He's never been around people, so you'll have to let him get used to you. But he's going to be a big one when he's grown. One that will tackle his weight in wildcats."

"I wouldn't want him to," I cuddled him under my chin, stroking his fur. For a minute he was tense, then he settled down and I even heard the beginning of a purr. I wondered what his purr would be like when he was grown, if all that noise could come from such a tiny thing.

"You like him?" asked Papa anxiously, and when I nodded, "What do you aim to name him?"

"How about Easter?" I asked. "It's next Sunday."

Papa looked doubtful.

"Somehow Easter should be for a dainty little female," he objected. "That cat will be a whopper. How about Cassius? You know, Cassius with the lean and hungry look?"

"He's not lean. He's fat. And he'll never be hungry," I promised. "Caesar's a nice name, though."

And that's how our new cat became Caesar. To tell you the truth I was ready for one by this time.

Antoinette had heard everything through the wall and was almost beside herself with excitement.

"Oh, I wish I could see him," she insisted when Papa was gone.

"If Papa's right, and he's a climber, you will," I promised. "A ten-foot wall won't stop him."

"I want to see him now. Now, when he's a kitten!"

"Maybe Sunday after next," I suggested. "We have to drive out to my Grandma and Grandpa's for the day. Maybe I could leave him with you."

Easter came, and it wasn't much. It never is. I had a new dress for Sunday school, pink dotted swiss, and everybody had new hats—or hats that looked like new. Sometimes they were last year's hats with new trimmings on them, but the congregation looked like a flower garden, and everyone was turning and twisting, trying to see what other people were wearing. There was a pot of hothouse lilies that had been brought from Salem on the altar and the rest of the church was decorated with so many garden flowers the sweetness almost made you sick.

It was the same old sermon, probably saved from last year, that I'd heard over and over. Easter was one time when you couldn't get away with just Sunday school. You had to stay for church, too.

Afterwards, we went home and there were all those Easter eggs staring at me. We'd dyed them yesterday, and that part was fun, but Easter eggs the second day are enough to turn your stomach. I wished there was a way I could get some through the wall to Antoinette, but I couldn't think of one. I couldn't throw them, or they'd break; I couldn't wash them down the millrace, because she'd already proved she couldn't catch anything and Papa had an eye out for the ladder. Besides they'd probably sink in the water.

"Oh, well," said Mama, who must have been thinking the same thing. "We can always use them in salads, and I can devil some of them."

"Maybe I could take a few to Mrs. Hutchinson and Miss Rebecca," I said with a sudden inspiration. "I bet they didn't color eggs."

"They'd probably throw them at you," said Papa.

"Maybe not," said Mama thoughtfully. "Marty's right. No one ever does anything for the Hutchinsons, and I'm sure they don't color eggs. Maybe if you just took them to the gate and knocked and when someone came say, 'Happy Easter,' it might be a pleasant surprise."

"It'll be a surprise, all right," said Papa. "If you want to try it, go ahead, but don't say I didn't warn you."

So Mama and I lined a berry box with grass and put in half a dozen hard boiled eggs. There were two blue ones, two pink ones, a purple and a yellow one, because they were the prettiest. Then, with my heart pounding like a drum, and trailed by Caesar, I went up the walk and crossed over to the gate in the Hutchinsons' wall.

After I rang the bell I waited a long time for an answer. Then I rang again. I was just about to leave when the gate swung back an inch or two and I saw Miss Rebecca's frightened eyes staring at me.

"What do you want?" she asked in a quavering voice.

"I brought you some Easter eggs." I was thankful it wasn't Mrs. Hutchinson who had opened the gate. "Here. Happy Easter. They're for you."

For a minute she hesitated, then a thin arm came out the opening and took the basket.

"Easter eggs," she said in a hushed whisper. "I haven't seen Easter eggs since I was a little girl."

"I hope you like them," I told her politely.

"Oh yes! We…I thank you very much."

And the door closed with a bang.

Spineless mouse! I thought as I walked home. I hope you get them to Antoinette before your mother sees them.

I didn't know how I could get Caesar across the wall to spend next Sunday with Antoinette. I'd spent all week off and on trying to teach him how to climb it and I've never seen a stupider cat. He just couldn't get the idea of climbing a wall. He could go up and down a tree perfectly well, but there was something about that wall he couldn't understand.

Finally I decided I'd just have to forget about my promise to Antoinette. There was no way to tell her, but when he wasn't there she'd know. Anyway, I hoped she'd got the eggs.

Chapter 10

SINCE WE HAD TO ALLOW for possible tire blowouts and the engine overheating, we left for Grandma and Grandpa's farm at seven-thirty in the morning.

I wanted to wear my overalls because they're more comfortable on a farm, but Mama insisted I wear a dress and shoes and stockings.

"You know your grandma," she reminded me. "She'd be shocked if you weren't correctly clothed on Sunday."

Papa backed the Model T out of the barn and drove it up to the house, where the engine died.

"I'm afraid it's flooded," he said apologetically. "We'll have to wait awhile for it to cool off."

"Good," I exclaimed. "It will give me time to get Caesar. He ran up a tree when he heard the car coming."

"Now, Marty," said Mama positively, "you are not to take that cat. Not to Grandma's. She's got plenty of animals of her own and besides he might run away and you'd never find him again."

"Then can I leave him in the house?" I asked. "He does use a paper. And he's so little. What if somebody should steal him?"

"Nobody's going to steal him," Papa assured me. "The town is full of kittens, and he's quite capable of taking care of himself for the day. He knows where he lives. Just put his food on the back porch and leave him out. He'll be all right."

I knew it wasn't any use arguing, particularly since Caesar was so high up in the apple tree I couldn't get him. He just sat there, bobbing his stump of a tail and glaring down at me. So finally I went back to the car.

Papa told us both to get in so we'd be ready. Then he pulled down the gas and the spark and went around front to crank. It took several turns before the engine finally caught, and it must have turned over hard because his face grew pretty red. As soon as it caught he rushed back to the driver's seat and readjusted the spark, and we knew we were ready to start.

Papa and Mama both had on automobiling clothes, long brown dusters. Papa had a cap and goggles and Mama had a veil that tied down over her hat. I only had an old cotton bathrobe to keep off the dust, and an old hat covered up my hair. Mama said I was growing so fast it was silly to buy something I'd outgrow by next summer, and it was all right with me. It would have been nice not to cover up at all with the wind whipping through the back seat the way it did. In the winter we had isinglass side curtains to put up, but in the summer we just enjoyed the wind or at least I did. It made me feel like we were going one hundred miles an hour instead of just twenty-five.

Grandpa's farm was only ten miles from town, but it seemed longer because the road was so winding. You couldn't see much of the country through the dust, which was hub-deep mud in the winter but rose like fine sand in the summer. We went along, jolting up and down. It was fun.

Once we met a car and had to back halfway down a hill until we could find a place wide enough for it to pass. And twice on steep hills the engine boiled over and we had to wait and let it cool off. Papa always carried a canteen of water for emergencies like that.

But at last we heard the geese and we knew that we were

there. The geese lived by the slough at Grandpa's farm, and he said they were better than watchdogs about letting him know when someone was coming. Of course, they weren't smart enough to know if it was a friend or an enemy, but they let out a clatter that you could hear for miles when anyone came down the road.

Grandma and Grandpa were waiting for us in rocking chairs on the front porch. They always sat there in summer even though you were expected to go in and out the door at the back. Only the preacher was invited to use the front door.

Grandma was a tall, bony lady with sandy-colored hair. Her hair used to be red, but it had faded, and now she washed it in sage tea to keep it from becoming gray. She would never have dreamed of dying it, any more than she would have used anything but a little cornstarch to keep the shine from her nose and high forehead. Sage tea and cornstarch were "nature" so they were all right. She had gray eyes that always seemed to be looking for my bad spots and sort of a gratey voice. I was a little scared of Grandma.

I wasn't scared of Grandpa, though. You couldn't see too much of him because of his hair. Grandma trimmed it herself, but there was so much of it that it covered his head like a sheep dog's. He had a moustache and a long white beard that hung down to his chest, but the brown eyes that looked out above all that hair were kind.

I knew without ever being told that Mama was Grandpa's favorite daughter and Aunt Gertrude was Grandma's. Nobody ever said so, but some things don't have to be explained.

"Well, you got here," said Grandpa. "Road pretty dusty, I reckon."

"It was dusty," agreed Papa.

"Take off your coats and caps and shake them over the

railing," advised Grandma. "Stay as clear from the porch as you can."

So we all took off our coats and veils and hats and shook as much dust as we could without getting any on Grandma's clean porch.

"Well, it's about time for old Shep to go to work," said Grandpa, when everyone had sat down again. "He's a little late today. Figured you might like to watch him earn his keep, Marty."

"Jim Morgan, you mean to tell me those cows ain't been put to pasture yet?" demanded Grandma sharply.

"I been waiting for Marty," said Grandpa mildly. "Come on, girl. There's something on the back porch you'd like to see, too."

"Well, I never!" Grandma was mad, but not too mad. She knew Grandpa would do as he pleased no matter how she felt. "Them cows are supposed to go to pasture 'bout six o'clock. And here they been waiting in the barn till nine. Just so a chit of a girl can watch a sheep dog work."

Papa got up and joined us, and I didn't blame him. Watching a sheep dog work was better than just sitting on the porch and visiting.

Shep was waiting on the back porch, his one blue eye and one brown eye—Grandpa always said a sheep dog with matched eyes wasn't worth a grain of salt—filled with anxiety. He jumped up happily when he saw us coming. "Now?" his violently wagging tail seemed to ask. "Now, can I do my job?"

"Just one minute, Shep," Grandpa told him tolerantly. "Look over there, Marty. Next to the wall."

All I could see was a round ball of black and white fur, but when I poked it gently, a head emerged and a pink tongue found and licked my hand.

"It's Shep Number Three," said Grandpa. "This here's Number Two and his daddy was Number One. Greatest dog I ever knew, though Number One was no slouch. Shep's getting old, though, so before he meets his maker I got him a puppy to train."

It was absolutely the cutest puppy I'd ever seen. Roly-poly, with tiny legs all but concealed by the soft fur. I looked carefully. Yes, there was a blue eye and a brown one. Then he closed them both and went back to sleep.

"He has the makings of a fine dog," said Papa admiringly.

"He's pretty young," explained Grandpa apologetically. "Got him soon as he could drink from a dish. About all you can expect from him now is sleep. But that's good too. It'll make him grow. All right, Shep. Get the cows and take them to pasture."

It was what Shep Number Two had been waiting for since early morning. With a happy yelp, he bounded toward the barn. There was a gate to pass through before he got there, but he mastered the bar that held it shut by standing on his hind legs and raising it with his nose. He handled the barn latching in the same way before he darted inside. One after another the cows came filing out, quickly at first, then slowing down as they reached the yard. They didn't linger there. Shep had them through the gate with a few short barks and one or two nips at a leg moving too slowly for his taste. Then he paused to close the gate bar before he escorted his charges down the lane.

"It's a half-mile to the pasture they're using now," said Grandpa. "Want to follow along and watch or have you had enough?"

"Oh yes," I told him eagerly. "That's the smartest dog I ever saw."

"No smarter than his pappy." I could see Grandpa was

pleased. "He trained him. Just like Shep will train Number Three when he's old enough."

"And who trained Number One?" asked Papa.

"I did," Grandpa told him proudly. "You think I'd let another man mess around one of my sheep dogs?"

The three of us trailed Shep and his charges down the dusty lane.

"He generally does this by himself," said Grandpa. "I don't bother to go along. And he brings them back at night the same way."

"You're lucky to have him," said Papa. "One of the smartest dogs I ever saw."

"Just a matter of training," said Grandpa modestly. "The horses are over here in this field. Want to have a look at them?"

So we looked at the sleek, healthy horses, the smelly pigs that had to be slopped and that stood in their food, getting it all over them, the turkeys, the chickens, which Grandpa said were Grandma's since she got all the butter and egg money. We didn't see the sheep because they were in a high pasture. But we saw the wheat and oats coming up in lines as straight as a ruler, the field of sprouting corn and the kitchen garden close to the house that was filled with greening stalks. It was hard to tell them apart except for the peas, which were already heavy with pods. But Papa knew and Grandpa was pleased that he did.

"Peas go in early. No later than Washington's birthday," said Papa knowledgeably and I looked at him in surprise. I had no idea he knew so much about a farm.

"Got mine in before that," admitted Grandpa, grinning. "About the ninth of February it was. We'll probably have some for dinner today."

Grandma was shouting something from the back porch. I couldn't understand, but Grandpa did.

"Time to feed the bummers. You'll like that, Marty."

A bummer is a lamb without a mother. Sometimes the mother has died. Or sometimes they just won't accept the baby. To keep the babies alive, they have to be fed four times a day from a bottle.

It wasn't as easy as it sounded. Grandpa got the clean bottles, filled them with cow's milk and put heavy nipples of black rubber on each one.

"You take one, Marty," he told me. "And hold your thumb tight over the flap. These lambs are mighty greedy."

"I can take two, one in each hand," I assured him.

The lambs, pushing their little black noses through the fence, were cute. They were covered with white curly wool, and because they knew what was going to happen, they tried to edge each other away. There were four of them, all little orphans.

"Start with one," advised Papa. "I'll feed one too, Jim. It's been years since I did this."

Grandpa gave us each a bottle and we held them up against the wire. Instantly they were grabbed and the lambs began sucking noisily. They sucked with such force that it was all I could do to hold onto the bottle, and I didn't see how Grandpa, who was feeding the third and fourth lambs, could hold onto two. Milk dripped from their mouths and down their chins, but they didn't care. All they wanted was to get it inside them as soon as possible. As fast as one had drained his bottle he tried to nudge out the lamb next to him in an effort to drink his share, too. It wasn't nearly as much fun as I thought it would be, and the lambs weren't as cute up close, either. I put my hand through the wire to pat mine on the head. Instead of a soft, downy cushion, their heads were hard and knobby.

On the way back to the house we passed the barn where

a load of baled hay had been dumped below the loft.

"You ought to get that inside, Jim," said Papa. "There's clouds blowing up from the south. It could rain by morning."

"It's going to rain all right. Probably a real soaker," said Grandpa. "But it was dark when I got that hay here yesterday. I told Martha I figured to pile it in the loft this morning and she most bust a pudding string. Today's the Lord's day and no work. Rain or no rain. Moldy hay or not, she'd skin me alive if she caught me at it."

"She wouldn't skin me," said Papa. "Many's the bale of hay I've stacked in a barn loft."

"On the Sabbath?"

"No. My folks were too religious for that. I was like you. I had to twiddle my thumbs on Sunday. But the way I see it, if somebody was to chuck it up there to me I could have it piled and out of the way in no time. Martha didn't tell you not to chuck those bales of hay, did she? Just not to pile it up."

"No. No, she didn't say nothing about that," agreed Grandpa, grinning. "But you run a chance of going to hell."

"Probably will anyway. And I'll meet a lot of old friends," said Papa cheerfully. "Now your job, Marty, is to keep your mama and grandma occupied. If it looks like they're heading for the barn, sound an alarm. If they ask where we are tell them we're probably sitting under a tree, swapping yarns. For all you know, we could be."

After a while Mama came out on the back porch and rang a big school bell, which made Shep Two wiggle all over with delight as he thought of the bones to come and awoke Shep Three so he stood up and stretched lazily. It was the signal for dinner.

Sunday dinner at Grandma's was always fried chicken. I was glad I hadn't been here earlier when she killed it. She'd pick out a likely rooster from the flock, put his head over a block and chop it off with an axe. The headless chicken always jumped around for a minute or two afterwards, and the first time I saw it happen I couldn't eat chicken for a month. Then she scalded it in boiling water, picked off the feathers, cleaned out the insides, cut it into pieces and fried it in bacon grease and lard. If you hadn't seen what went before, Grandma's chicken was wonderful, and she said all farm women did the same thing. There were always more roosters than laying hens in a batch of chicks, and you shouldn't have more than one rooster in a flock or they'd fight, so it was best to eat them.

Besides the chicken, there were boiled potatoes and cream gravy made with chicken fat; fresh peas from the garden; corn that wasn't fresh but tasted that way because Grandma had dried it and then boiled it; kale, which I never could stand but was one of the vegetables left in the winter root cellar; baking powder biscuits with your choice of wild honey or quince preserves; pickles; chow chow and two kinds of pie, dried apple or custard. I ate until I was full to my chin.

Grandpa pushed back his chair.

"What say we go lay out under the apple tree, Sam?" he suggested. "That one up the other side of the barn is old and the apples don't amount to much. But it's nice and shady."

"Not till you feed your dog," cried Grandma, jumping up. "I'll scrape the plates, then you go tend to him. He's hanging round the back door like a fly."

She scraped everything from our once heaped plates into Shep's dish, chicken and bones, potatoes, gravy, vegetables, even the crusts of pie, and gave it to Grandpa. He carried it outside and put it down where Shep received it thankfully. He was twelve years old and had been dining on similar fare every Sunday since he was a puppy.

Mama and Grandma did the dishes, while I put them

away. I wasn't going to until Grandma made a biting remark about idle hands, so I guessed I'd better.

"You want to go back outside?" asked Grandma. "Never know who might pass by on the road."

"It's getting hot," objected Mama. "I think I'd rather stay in."

"Well, I guess, since you're company we could sit in the parlor," said Grandma reluctantly. "It probably could stand an airing out anyway."

The layout of Grandma's house was simple, like most farmhouses. There was a narrow hall that led from the front door to the back, and it was carpeted with a braided rag rug she had made herself, using the good portions of worn out clothing. On the left was the company bedroom and behind it the stairway that led up to two bedrooms and an attic. I didn't care to go up there because the small paned windows were nailed shut. They were never opened, winter or summer, but Grandma and Grandpa, who slept up there, didn't seem to notice.

The company bedroom also had a handmade woven rug and contained a maple bed, a chest of drawers and a dressing table with ledges on either side of the mirror for candles and a compartment for the chamber pot below. It would have been bad manners to leave the chamber pot under the bed where anyone could see it.

The kitchen was in the back of the house, across the hall from the stairs, with Grandma's immaculately scrubbed milk room off the back porch. The dining room was in front of the kitchen, with the parlor in front of that, to the right of the front door.

I hadn't been in the parlor many times because the doors were always closed, maybe even locked. It was dusky because Grandma kept the blinds down. That was to save the color of the pink roses, as big as cabbages, in the only store-boughten rug in the house. There were six straight-backed walnut chairs with cane seats around the walls, a small table in the center of the room that held the big family Bible with all our names in it, and a walnut pump organ in the corner by the window. All the windows had white curtains edged with tatting and there was a tatting-trimmed cloth on the center table.

Grandma, who was making more tatting, sat in one of the straight-backed chairs and Mama in another.

"Maybe I'll play the organ," said Mama. She sounded a little nervous.

"So long as you play hymns," agreed Grandma. "It's the Sabbath. Remember the Sabbath and keep it holy."

"Then how can you tat?" asked Mama.

"Tatting's not work," said Grandma. "I do it without thinking. Mending now—I wouldn't dream of tackling a basket of mending on the Sabbath."

So Mama opened up the organ and played *Rock of Ages* and *Abide With Me* and *Little Brown Church* and a lot of other songs that we sang in Sunday school. I listened to the sound of the ocean in the big pink sea shell that someone had given Grandma and she prized most of everything she owned. And I pulled off some of the feathery fronds from one of the dried pampas grasses she had set in a vase. I only pulled the back ones that didn't show. Then, when I didn't know what to do with them, I put them in my pocket.

Finally, Mama closed the organ and stood up.

"I think it's time we started home," she said. "It's after three o'clock. What if we had a blowout? It would take Sam till after dark to fix it."

"I'll get him," I offered quickly. "You stay here and rest, Mama."

"How is your female complaint, Bea?" Grandma asked as I went out the door. "Now if you'd only take my advice—"

Papa and Grandpa were working away at the hay. I couldn't believe how many bales they'd managed to get inside the loft.

"Mama wants to go home," I told them breathlessly.

"We better quit," said Grandpa, leaning on his pitch fork. "But I'm beholden to you, Sam."

"There's only a few more to go," Papa reminded him. "Half an hour maybe."

"You don't know Martha." Grandpa sighed. "She'd be out here hollering her head off. No, we best leave them. Though now I can spread a tarp and keep off the worst of the rain."

As we walked back to the house Papa and Grandpa were talking and joking in a way I'd never seen them do before.

After they stopped at the pump and washed up, they were still red and perspiring when we got inside the house.

"Thought you was going to sit in the shade," said Grandma, looking at them sharply.

"My fault," Papa told her. "The sun felt so good that I talked Jim into sitting in the open. I don't get enough sun in my line of work."

Mama opened her mouth, then closed it again. She knew Papa got lots of sun. The only thing she said was after we were in the car and the engine was making so much noise it drowned her out. "What were you doing, anyway, Sam? You smell like on old horse."

"Loading hay."

"It does look like it is going to blow up a rain," said Mama jerkily. We'd hit a lot of wagon ruts in the road. "I hope you got it all in."

As soon as we got home I started looking for Caesar. I looked in all the places he liked best and called and called, but he didn't answer.

"He's gone. He's run away. Somebody stole him." I tried to think of all the dreadful things that could have happened to my yellow kitten.

"He's got to be around here somewhere." Mama was still putting away things that Grandma had insisted on sending home with us: almost a side of bacon, a long string of her own dried apples to make pies, a pot of butter she had churned, another of honey from a tree Grandpa had cut down, a mess of green peas, a loaf of freshly baked bread and I don't know what-all.

"I'll help you look," offered Papa. "He's probably asleep somewhere under a bush and doesn't hear your call."

Just then there was a knock on the door. When Papa opened it. Miss Rebecca was standing there holding Caesar in her hands.

"Is this your cat?" she asked timidly.

I rushed forward and grabbed him. He promptly bit me.

"He's ours all right," agreed Papa dryly. "Though he doesn't seem happy to be home. Where did you find him?"

"He must have come over the wall," said Miss Rebecca breathlessly. "When we got home from church, there he was. My little—I mean, I thought I'd seen him here so I kept him in my room till you got home. You see, my mother doesn't like cats."

Without further explanation she turned and was gone, but I wondered how Antoinette had managed to coax Caesar over the wall.

Chapter 11

THE NEXT WEEK a terrible thing happened. When I came home from school Mrs. Hershy was in her front yard training up her sweet peas and she called to me.

"Oh, Marty! Ain't it dreadful? Ain't it just awful? I can't help thinking what if it had been Ralphie!"

"What's awful, Mrs. Hershy? What's happened?"

"Why Glen French has been killed! Didn't you know? His folks got the telegram just this afternoon."

Glen French was Andy's best friend. I'd known him all my life, and suddenly I got a sick feeling in the middle of my stomach.

"There must be some mistake, Mrs. Hershy!" I said sharply. "He was with Andy, fighting in the trenches. I'm sure they dug them deep enough to be safe."

"Well, this time they didn't. You know, young people get careless. That's why I'm so thankful that Ralphie never got sent overseas. I guess they realized he'd be more valuable right here in the quartermaster's office."

I didn't want to hear any more. I ran home as fast as I could. Mama's eyes were all pink so I knew she'd already heard.

"Oh, Mama! What if it had been Andy? And why did it have to be Glen? He was a good boy. Why, once he even danced with me when I asked him to at the county fair. Andy wouldn't. He told me to run along and grow up, but Glen didn't. Some of the big girls laughed, but he didn't care."

Mama sat down in the rocking chair and I sat on her lap, though I was so big it wasn't very comfortable.

"Maybe there's a mistake?" I suggested tearfully.

"I'm afraid not. The telegram said a letter would follow."

"But he must have been right next to Andy in that trench. Maybe it killed him too."

"We would have heard," said Mama a little too firmly.

"Boche! Hun! Kraut! Barbarian!" I shouted all the terrible names people called the Germans and Mama didn't try to stop me. Maybe she was thinking the same thing.

In a few days the letter came from Glen's commanding officer, and we knew there was no mistake. A shell had landed in the trench and Glen had been killed instantly. Luckily there were no other casualties, although one soldier, who had been next to him, had been sent to the hospital for shock. We all knew who that soldier was. Andy! Papa called everyone he could think of who had anything to do with the war, but he couldn't find out anything.

I'd never worried about my cousin before, but now I was really worried about him. I didn't see him very often, but I didn't want anything to happen to Andy. As for the towns-people, they were hopping mad. We had already lost too many boys from a town the size of Maple Glen and they didn't like it.

Since they wouldn't be bringing Glen home, there was a memorial service for him on Sunday, but Mama said I didn't have to go if I didn't want to. I didn't see how it could do him any good if I went so I didn't. But everybody else in town did. Even Papa. People were standing out in the streets because there wasn't room for them inside the church. I just stayed home and thought about how nice Glen had always been to me and that we'd never see him again. I thought about Andy, too, and hoped they were taking good care of him in that hospital.

I told Antoinette all about it and she was very sympathetic. Then I had to tell her about the war. She didn't even know there was one going on. I guess Miss Rebecca and Mrs. Hutchinson didn't talk to her very much.

The next Sunday was May 30, Decoration Day. Mrs. Hutchinson would be going out to the Pioneers Cemetery instead of going to church, and so would we, so I couldn't talk to Antoinette. We always did the same thing on Decoration Day. Early in the morning, Mama would pick the nicest flowers in the yard and wrap them up in wet newspapers. Then she'd collect a lot of tin cans—this was a little hard because cans were one of the things we were supposed to turn over to the Red Cross.

"But after the flowers wilt somebody can come along and collect the cans to turn in," Mama assured us. "We can't have the flowers dying."

Then she peeled the labels off the cans so they were pretty and shiny and got a heavy spatula and trowel. The spatula was to scrape moss off tombstones and the trowel to dig out weeds on the graves. She packed a big picnic lunch and she was ready to go.

Papa and I had been ready a long time. All we needed were two buckets with handles and we'd already put them in the Ford.

We got a little later start than usual this year because Mama thought we ought to put in our appearance at the parade.

I thought the whole thing was a bore. It started at nine o'clock and was led by a drum and bugle corps. They were old men, Civil War veterans, who didn't play very well, but they looked proud in their faded uniforms. After this came the remaining members of the Grand Army of the Republic. There weren't very many of them, maybe a dozen, and they too wore their blue uniforms, which didn't fit very well. One of the veterans had to be wheeled in a chair, but he looked as proud as any of them. Then came four members of the Rebel Army in gray uniforms. Since they had lost the war there had been a lot of criticism when they first wanted to march. But the city council finally decided they could come if they didn't carry a Rebel flag and no one could have looked prouder than those four old men. After that came the Veterans of the Spanish American war. They were younger, and they looked sort of impatient because they had to walk so slowly. But the old men were doing the best they could. After that came the mayor, riding a horse, and then the high school band, walking very carefully so they wouldn't step in anything the horse left behind, and a half-dozen decorated automobiles with flags sticking out the window and bunting on the sides.

"Gets fewer every year," said Papa regretfully as the old soldiers passed. "One of these days there won't be any of them left. You want to go out to the city cemetery, Bea? And listen to the speeches?"

"We'd better not," she decided. "The moss was thick on the trees this year, which means it will be heavy on the monuments. I'll have my work cut out for me."

So once more Papa cranked up the flivver (which was what most people except Mama called our Model T Ford) and we were on our way.

The Pioneer Cemetery, where my great-grandparents were buried, was about four miles from town. There were a lot of other Burnhams and Morgans buried there, too, though I didn't know who most of them were. I did know about Uncle Ned, Grandma's brother, who hanged himself in the barn one day. I never could find out why. I'd heard it was because his wife, Great-Aunt Dorcas, was such a nag, but I couldn't get anyone to admit it, even Mrs. Hershy. Great-Aunt Dorcas's headstone was right next to Uncle Ned's though, so he never managed to get away from her. Alongside were some of their children, mostly babies.

It was a very interesting cemetery even if it was only kept up once a year. It was on a hill and the tombstones were all kinds. Some opened like a book, with poetry on the leaves, some had marble baby lambs on the top, one even had a carved angel. Some were very tall, some were shorter and square. A few had iron chain fences marking them off, and one of these was for two babies, twins, I suppose, who must have died when they were born.

The Hutchinsons had already arrived and Miss Rebecca was on a ladder, scraping moss from the top of her father's monument. Of course, they'd left Antoinette at home and I hoped she wasn't expecting me. The Hutchinson monument was tall, like a spire of polished gray marble, and there was a lion on top. It was the grandest in the whole cemetery, but it took a lot of care.

Miss Rebecca was teetering on the top of a ten-foot ladder, clutching at the marble while she scraped moss from the lion. Her mother stood at the bottom, giving orders and occasionally reaching out to hold the ladder.

I stopped short, staring at them. I hadn't known the Hutchinsons had so tall a ladder. But now that I knew, everything became perfectly plain to me. Antoinette could climb up her side, then down our ladder and she would be safe. Once she saw Mama and Papa she wouldn't be scared anymore. And once they saw her—well, Papa could do anything. That was how she could escape.

Some men had brought scythes and were already clearing away the grass and wild roses and blackberries and myrtle that had grown up between the headstones, but Papa never brought a scythe.

"These men are expert," he always said. "I'd just get in their way."

Mama went straight to the plot marked Morgan where her grandparents were buried. The monument was polished marble with a kind of speckled design. One side said "Mother," the other "Father." I didn't think it was very pretty compared with some of the others, but it was big.

"Just look at that moss," Mama exclaimed. "I had every bit cleaned off last year, but it's grown back an inch."

Papa gave me a wink and we went to get our buckets. The hill behind the cemetery was filled with wild strawberries. You could hardly step for walking on them. Until you'd eaten one, you couldn't imagine how good warm wild strawberry pie covered with cream could be. That was our job on Decoration Day, though some people didn't approve.

"It's like robbing the graves," somebody told us once.

"Dear lady," said Papa, "the dead wouldn't deny us this delicious fruit. They're too full of nectar and ambrosia to care about a few earthly strawberries."

Today the men with the scythes had got there so early we couldn't pick on top but had to go down the slope where there weren't any graves.

We didn't meet anyone on the slope but Miss Edna Pope and I felt guilty the minute I saw her. She had a basket of flowers over one arm.

"Morning, Edna," called Papa cheerily. "Fine day."

"Morning, Judge," said Miss Edna, but her eyes were on me and she wasn't smiling.

"Morning, Miss Edna," I said, and I felt my cheeks burning. "I'm still coming to see you one of these days. I asked Mama and she said it would be fine."

"She did?" She was smiling now and looking almost pretty.

"What's this?" asked Papa curiously. "Marty's not been bothering you, has she, Edna?"

"Oh no. No indeed," said Miss Edna quickly. "I have a lot of scraps left over from dressmaking and I told Marty to stop by and I'd give them to her. She didn't ask, Judge; I offered."

"And she's going to help me sew," I told him. "Mama was very pleased about that."

"I should think so," said Papa. "I should warn you, Edna, Marty's a wiggle worm. Doesn't like to sit down too long at a time. Always on the go."

"I'll come as soon as school's out," I promised. "It's just that I've been so busy."

"I understand," said Miss Edna, smiling again as she started up the hill to the plot where her mother and grand-parents were buried.

"Poor Edna," said Papa, looking after her. "She's had a mighty hard time of it living here. She never had any friends that I know of and children can be mighty unkind. But she stuck it out, and now I understand she can snap her fingers at any of them. You go and see her, Marty, since she asked you. I never heard of her asking anyone to her house before."

"I will, Papa," I promised. "Just as soon as I get time. I think she's nice. Why didn't she leave Maple Glen anyway? I would have."

"Stubborn, maybe," said Papa. "But this is the way she wants to live, and she's doing it."

"If you were her, wouldn't you have left a long time ago? She could have got a job sewing anywhere."

"Yes, ma'am," he agreed. "But I'm not as brave as Edna Pope."

"Would there have been some place for her to go if she'd wanted to run away when she was a little girl?"

"There's always the orphanage," said Papa thoughtfully. "But Mrs. Pope, Edna's grandma, was a mighty loving woman. And her grandpa was a good man. I reckon they made her feel wanted, and after all, they were family. I don't know why she stayed on when they were gone, though."

I thought about it all the time I was filling my bucket with berries. It was plain that Antoinette wasn't loved or wanted. Somewhere she had to have a father. Maybe he was a loving man.

Chapter 12

THE INVITATION WAS WRITTEN on white paper with gold ink and there was a little gold sticker on top. Papa brought it home from the post office and handed it to me when I arrived for lunch.

"What is it, Marty?" asked Mama as I stood staring at it.

I handed it to her without saying anything.

"Why it's an invitation to a masquerade party," she exclaimed in a pleased tone. "Mrs. Chenoworth is giving a masquerade party for Eldon on his thirteenth birthday. It's June six, from seven-thirty to ten P.M. and Mr. Chenoworth will call for the children and bring them home."

"There's a war going on," said Papa frowning. "It's no time to waste sugar and eggs on a birthday cake. Maybe they'll even have ice cream too."

"Of course they'll have ice cream," said Mama. "Whoever heard of a birthday party without? Let's see now—why, the sixth is next Saturday. We'll have to start thinking of a costume right away."

"There'll be boys there," pointed out Papa. "Marty is too young for a party with boys. Marty's only twelve. And ten o'clock is too late. She goes to bed at nine."

"She'll be thirteen this fall," Mama reminded him. "She can't spend the rest of her life going to parties with nothing but girls. And the Chenoworths will be there. She'll be well chaperoned. Besides, it won't hurt her to stay up one hour late."

"I don't like it," said Papa grumpily. "In the first place it's at night. She's never been to a party at night before, or one with boys."

"Now, Sam, you sound like you're jealous," said Mama smiling. "You'll just have to make up your mind your little girl is growing up. I admit that I'd rather they put it off till next year when Marty will be in the eighth grade, but I know Marie Chenoworth must have her reasons."

"She has." It was the first time I'd spoken. "The boys don't like Eldon very much. He's a sissy."

"Does that mean you don't want to go?" asked Papa quickly.

"No, I want to go," I admitted after I'd thought about it a minute. "I wouldn't want to be left out."

"Oh, Marie would never do that," said Mama. "She probably asked the whole seventh grade to Eldon's party."

But Mrs. Chenoworth hadn't. Fay hadn't received one of the white and gold invitations. In fact only four seventh grade girls, including me, had. Barbara Simmons, whose father owned the biggest prune orchard and drier in the state and whose grandmother had crossed the plains with mine; Marian Delaney, whose father was district attorney; Claire Webster, whose father owned Webster's Grocery Store. There were only three seventh grade boys, leaving Eldon to make up the fourth, but in addition Mrs. Chenoworth had invited eight kids from the eighth grade. I knew them all and saw them every year at the Pioneer Picnic in the park, which Grandma always made us attend.

I guess I'd better stop right here and explain a little about Maple Glen. It wasn't any different from the other Willamette Valley towns I'd heard of. Nobody ever came right out and talked about it, but it was divided into classes. At the top were the descendents of pioneers, only that wasn't quite enough. These descendents had to have respectable positions, not like Henry Riggs who lived by doing pick-up work, although his grandparents were just as much pioneers as anyone. Just below them were the later arrivals who had money. They invested it in business and made more, but they were still on the fringe because they couldn't brag about the troubles of their grandparents crossing the plains. At the bottom were the millworkers and newcomers. And there were none of these on Mrs. Chenoworth's list.

The Chenoworth's were in the second class, but Mrs. Chenoworth wanted to be number one. Her husband was the town banker, and since they couldn't go to the Pioneer Picnics, she had taken care to invite only those who could to Eldon's party.

Mama never talked about such things, but Aunt Gertrude did. She was always saying it was too bad Mrs. Chenoworth came from the Middle West, where nobody knew who her grandfather was.

I thought it was pretty silly and at recess I played with the kids from milltown whenever they were doing something interesting and I wanted to. Nobody said anything. Since Mama wouldn't let me fight with my fists anymore, I'd learned to fight with my tongue. I know I said mean things to people, and I almost wished I wouldn't, but somebody had to stick up for the millworkers' kids.

I walked through town that afternoon with Fay Phipps and almost at once she began talking about Eldon's party.

"Maybe I did get an invitation and it got mixed up in the mail," she said. "Was the envelope very small?"

"Smaller than the regular size." I knew she wouldn't get one, not that her grandparents weren't pioneers. Before prohibition came to Oregon, which was one of the earliest states to have it, Fay's grandpa had owned and operated the local saloon. He was too old to work now, but Maple Glen never forgot. A saloon keeper wasn't acceptable to the Chenoworths.

"I'm going to stop by the post office and see if it came in," she declared.

"I'd better not wait," I told her. I didn't want to see how disappointed she would be. "Mama told me to hurry home today."

"Okey-doke," she agreed. "I'll see you tomorrow then."

Mama was standing at the dining room table when I got there. It was piled with worn-out bed sheets. We'd had some of them so long that they were yellowed with age, but they had all been washed and ironed by Yuey Kim's patient hands.

"I've been thinking about your costume," said Mama when I came in. "Material's so expensive these days. But here's this stack of perfectly good sheets. All we'd have to do would be to cut out the worn spots. How would you like to be the Statue of Liberty?"

I said I wouldn't.

"I suppose we could dye them," she admitted. "Although I've never had good luck at dyeing. It always streaks. How about a ghost?"

"I don't want to wear a bed sheet. Barbara's mother is buying material to make her a Bo Peep costume. And Marjory's going to be a gypsy, with a long black skirt and lots of beads and gold earrings."

"I could make you a pinafore out of this one," said Mama. "It's hardly yellowed at all. And you could wear your blue recital dress with your hair down. And short white socks and your Mary Jane slippers and say you were Alice in Wonderland."

"I don't even want to think about a costume right now," I insisted. "I'll think of something later. Right now I want to... I want to call on Miss Edna Pope. I promised her a long time ago that I would."

Edna Pope was a spur of the moment excuse. I had forgotten her again, and all I really wanted was to get away from that pile of old bed sheets. Maybe I wouldn't go to the party at all. I wasn't feeling very good about it.

"Very well." Mama's eyes were reproachful. "But remember I'm not a fast seamstress, Marty. You'll have to make up your mind very soon. The party's next Saturday."

I felt bad about being so cross with Mama, but I didn't want to go to Eldon's party wearing a sheet. All the eighth grade girls would laugh, and so would the seventh graders. And being Alice in Wonderland wasn't right either. Everybody had seen my recital dress, and there I'd be in a pinafore made from a sheet.

When I got to Miss Edna's house I forgot about it though. She was so glad to see me. Nobody had ever acted so glad before. She took me straight to the kitchen for cookies and milk.

The cookies were oatmeal and very fresh. The milk was just milk.

"Now, did you bring your doll?" asked Miss Edna, getting up to refill the cookie plate.

"No, ma'am not this time. You see I have so many."

"Very good." She approved. "You need to see the size of the scraps you'll have to work with. I'm afraid they aren't very big. The customers always take the big ones away, though I don't know what they'll ever do with them. Wait here. I'll get them."

She came back with two bulging pillowcases and dumped their contents on the kitchen table. I had never seen such a mixture of beautiful colors in my life. Green taffeta, red and purple satin, yellow, pink, blue and gold. Every shade was there, although as she had said, in small pieces cut from neck and sleeve holes and strips with the selvage. In addition there were scraps of lace and ribbon and little bits of net with sequins on it. I stared and stared, almost afraid to touch anything, they were so beautiful.

"Well," said Miss Edna practically. "Anything there you can use? As you can guess, most of it came from my Salem customers. Maple Glen doesn't go in for such frills."

Gently I picked up a bit of scarlet velvet, feeling the soft texture with my fingers.

"I wish I had some of this," I told her. "Yards and yards of it. I'd go as Madam Pompadour. Then no one would laugh at me."

"Go? Where would you go, Marty? And who would laugh at you?"

"Eldon Chenoworth's having a masquerade party Saturday night. I have to have a costume. And Mama wants to make one out of an old bed sheet. She says I could be the Statue of Liberty or a ghost."

"I see," said Miss Edna thoughtfully. "Seems to me an old sheet's a splendid basis for a costume. No sense buying new material for just one night. There's other things that lend themselves to white besides ghosts and statues, though."

"What?" All the way there I'd been trying to think of something, but I couldn't.

"How about a bride?" she asked. "I think there's an old lace curtain of Grandma's somewhere. It would make a lovely veil."

"A bride?" Brides wore white! I looked at Miss Edna with admiration.

"Would it look like a bed sheet?" I asked anxiously.

"Not when I get through with it," she told me.

"But I couldn't ask you to…and I have to put all my money into thrift stamps."

"You're not asking me. I'm offering. And naturally I wouldn't take anything for it. Why I could whip up a bride's gown in a couple of hours. It wouldn't have to have finished seams underneath. Not for a costume."

"But do you have a pattern? Mama would buy one, I know."

"Never use a pattern," Miss Edna told me, sniffing. "Just measurements. Now stand up and let me see how big you are."

Chapter 13

MAMA WAS AMAZED WHEN I told her Miss Edna had offered to make me a costume.

"She's dreadfully expensive, Marty. I don't think we can afford it."

"She doesn't want any money. She said so. Just the bed sheet to work with."

Papa came home just then, and when he heard the story he sort of smiled.

"Let her do it, Bea," he advised. "When old man Pope died I settled the estate and didn't send a bill. Edna's just trying to pay her debt."

So the next day I carried the best of the bed sheets to school, carefully concealed in newspaper wrapping. I wouldn't tell anyone what they were either. I just said it was something I had to deliver after school.

The people who had been invited to Eldon's party could talk of nothing else but what they were going to wear. I wouldn't tell anyone about my costume. I wanted it to be a surprise. At recess the girls all got together to talk, and you could hear them all over the school grounds.

I stayed with Fay, who as I thought hadn't received an invitation after all.

"I should worry, I should care, I should marry a millionaire," she said over and over. "I never did like parties anyway and Eldon Chenoworth's such a dodo. His will probably be bad news."

She waited to walk partway home with me and I wished she hadn't because I had to turn off at Miss Edna's street.

"Where are you going?" Fay asked suspiciously.

"I've got to stop by the Popes'," I told her. "I've got to deliver this." I tapped my newspaper bundle.

"What is it?"

"Just some material," I told her airily.

"Is Edna Pope making a dress for your mama?" There was awe in Fay's tone.

"No," I admitted. Then after a minute I decided I might as well make a clean breast of it. She'd find out soon enough anyway. "For me. Miss Edna's making my costume for Eldon's party."

"Well, aren't you the cat's meow!" she said finally. "You go right ahead. Don't let me stop you." And she started running down the street.

I stared after her, wishing I had explained about Miss Edna paying back her debt to Papa and about Mama's bed sheets. Even if Miss Edna made the costume, it would still be made of old sheets.

There was a strange automobile sitting in front of Miss Edna's house, so I hung around waiting for her customer to leave. Pretty soon she did, a strange lady in a long automobile duster with her hat tied down by a veil. She must have been someone from Salem. I waited till she drove away, then I knocked on the door.

Miss Edna's welcome was as cordial as yesterday's.

"You brought them," she said, with a glance at my bundle. "Bring them right into the kitchen. I need a good light to see the worn spots so I can cut around them. If you like you can look at some of my new fashion magazines. They just came today in the morning's mail."

There was a whole stack of the magazines, all filled with pictures of ladies wearing fashionable dresses. I didn't know there were so many magazines like that. Raubeck's Mercantile Store only carried the Delineator and the Butterick. In shelves behind the counter there were patterns that went with them. You were lucky if you could find the size of pattern that you wanted. Raubeck's only carried two of each.

"Have you found anything you like?" asked Miss Edna when she finished inspecting the sheets for holes and tears.

"I can't find any brides."

"Over here. In the back." She flipped the pages, and rows of brides stared up at me. They were all beautiful and I said so.

"Hmph," said Miss Edna. "The same old thing. What you need is something brand new. Now here—" She paused on the second page. "This is very smart. Look at all the fullness in the skirt. You'll find nothing like it in Maple Glen—or Salem for that matter, but by fall everyone will be wearing them."

The dress was certainly different. The skirt was very full, not skimpy the way they had been. It was short, too. It came to at least two inches above the lady's ankles. It was sort of draped in front, and the hem was scalloped. The top was a lot like a petticoat with beads sewn on it. It didn't have any sleeves, only wide bands across each shoulder so you could see a lot of the lady. It must have taken yards of material to make, and I was glad that Mama had plenty of sheets.

"Now that is something new in styles," announced Miss Edna. "Unless you'd rather go back to the conventional wedding dress with a long skirt and short sleeves."

"Oh no," I decided instantly. How fine it would be to be the first one in Maple Glen to start a style.

"Good," agreed Miss Edna in satisfaction. "Then I'll get to work. Mrs. Forbes from Salem was just here but I told her I had another gown to do first and I couldn't get to her for a few days. She grumbled a little, but she'll wait."

Miss Edna unfolded the best sheet, got out my measurements, which she had written down, her scissors and a tape measure. Pretty soon she was slashing away at the bed sheet. Without a pattern to follow, I didn't see how it could come out right.

"Maybe I'd better go," I suggested. "Unless you need me."

"No, run along," she agreed absently. "I can't talk when I'm cutting, but be sure to come back tomorrow for a fitting."

The next day Fay spread it all over the school that Edna Pope was making my costume. You could see some of the kids were jealous and thought I was putting on airs. One or two were openly envious and wished they could have Miss Edna, too.

"It's bound to be pretty," said Barbara Simmons. "It will probably win the prize. I thought my Bo Peep dress would win because my mother sews so well. But not as well as Edna Pope. Nobody does."

"It's just made from old bed sheets." Barbara was so nice that I wanted to tell her.

She laughed.

"It won't look like it when Miss Pope gets through with it," she insisted. "Mama looked around for a bed sheet for my costume, but she'd given all our old ones to the Red Cross."

I made a mental note to tell Mama. Probably she didn't

know the Red Cross wanted old sheets. It's a wonder Aunt Gertrude hadn't told her.

I wished I could tell Antoinette about the party. She'd be so excited. I must remember every little thing that happened because she'd want to know, but Sunday was almost a week away.

Every day I had fittings, but I couldn't see how the dress would look because it wasn't put together.

"I'm grateful that I had your costume to practice on, Marty," she said. "Now when the ladies appear in the fall wanting new evening gowns, it will be no trouble to turn one out."

On Friday I picked up the dress. My, but it was beautiful, and I was almost sorry I'd told Barbara that it had started out as a sheet. She hadn't told anyone though, and I was thankful for that.

It had pearls sewed onto the top part and the shoulder bands and scattered around the skirt. Well, almost pearls, because they came from the Five and Dime Store, and Miss Edna had added a few touches of her own. Around each pearl she had sewed a frill of lace from her scrap bag. The lace didn't match, because it was just scraps, but the effect was wonderful and made the pearls look like the center of a flower.

When I carried it home and tried it on for my family, Papa raised his eyebrows.

"Where's the top?" he asked. "You're certainly not going out in public that way!"

"It is just beautiful," said Mama. "Edna Pope is an artist. I wouldn't wear it myself, but it looks lovely on Marty, Sam, and if Edna says it's the new style, we know it is."

"We'll have to take Edna's word about the style," admitted Papa. "I know she did her best for you."

The evening of the party I put it on again, and for the first time thought about my feet. The lady in the magazine had white shoes with high heels that matched her dress. All I had was my Sunday Mary Janes with a strap across the instep.

"They look just horrible!" I cried, staring down at the slippers. "They look like baby shoes. I need high heels."

"Not at your age," said Papa firmly. "You've got to take care of your feet."

"Perhaps a new coat of vaseline would bring out the shine," suggested Mama. "Even if I wanted to loan you a pair of my shoes they wouldn't fit."

"What good would that do? You don't wear high heels," I wailed. "The bride in the picture did."

"Stop whining," ordered Papa. "That's one thing I don't tolerate. A whining child."

Then there was a knock at the door.

"It's Eldon," I cried. "Tell him I can't go. Tell him I'm sick."

"I'll do nothing of the kind," said Papa. "You accepted an invitation, you have a costume, and now you'll go." He had forgotten how he didn't want me to go to a girl-boy party in the first place.

"Take your sweater." Mama picked my blue one up from the chair where I had dumped it earlier. "It may be chilly at ten when you come home. And here's your present."

Present! I had forgotten it was a birthday party. They always called for presents. Mama must have picked out something and wrapped it up in white paper and blue ribbon. It was square and flat and thin, so it couldn't be a cup and saucer, which is what we generally took to girls' parties. Or at least we used to. There hadn't been many parties since the war, and we wouldn't have taken little cups and saucers if there were. They had Prussia stamped in gold underneath the cups.

I stuck the package under one arm and my parents literally pushed me ahead of them out the door. While they were greeting Eldon, who was dressed as a doctor, I got myself together and tried to forget about my Mary Janes sticking out below my skirt. Then I thought about walking with my legs scrooched down and my knees bent. It made the hem of the skirt almost touch the ground. It was hard to do, but at least nobody could see my hateful Mary Janes and white ribbed stockings. I put on my little white domino mask that all the girls had agreed to wear to the party as we went down the walk.

"Why are you walking so slow?" asked Eldon when we were halfway to the gate. "Have I got leprosy that you're afraid to walk with me?"

"It's my dress," I told him with dignity. "All the ladies will be wearing dresses like this before long." I readjusted the veil that Miss Edna had made from her grandmother's old lace curtain. It was a very nice veil with a circle of artificial flowers around my head.

"Oh," said Eldon respectfully. "I heard that Edna Pope was making your costume, but nobody seemed to know what you were going to be."

"A June bride."

"Some bride," Eldon admitted. "You sure look like the cat's whiskers." That was a compliment, but I wished it had come from somebody else. Eldon Chenoworth looked a little like a white slug.

It was hard getting into the back seat of the Chenoworths' car, but I did it. Barbara Simmons was already there—I could tell by her costume—and two boys who wore full masks and were dressed like Abraham Lincoln and a policeman.

"I'm glad you came," whispered Barbara, clutching my arm. "It was embarrassing sitting here alone with two boys."

"Papa had to make three trips," said Eldon from the front seat, which, besides his father, was occupied by a red devil with horns. "We can't get everybody at once. The car won't hold them, even if it is a Chalmers."

"That's okey-doke," said Abraham Lincoln. I recognized the voice. It was Freddy Taylor, so the policeman was probably Orville Dunn, since they lived next door to each other.

The Chenoworths lived on what we call "The Hill." It's a quarter of a mile from town, which isn't far when you consider I walk a mile each noon from school to home and back after lunch, but to hear the Chenoworths talk, it was like living in another town. Eldon's father drove him to school each morning and his mother picked him up afterward.

They had a big house with a huge living room and lots of furniture, only it had all been pushed against the wall.

"To make room for games," explained Mrs. Chenoworth gaily as she met us at the door, "and maybe even dancing. Eldon goes to Salem once week for lessons and I'm sure he'll be able to show you the foxtrot. It's the very newest thing."

Nobody said anything. The seventh grade didn't dance, not really, and while the eighth grade had a graduation dance I'd heard it was pretty terrible.

Mrs. Chenoworth recovered herself quickly.

"The girls may leave their wraps in the guest room, right here," she said pointing to a closed door. "If the boys have any—but I see you haven't."

Barbara and I took our sweaters into the room she showed us and put them on the bed with the other girls' wraps. It was a very elegant room with a bed made of solid brass, a dressing table with three mirrors so you could see both sides of your face at once, a chiffonier made of the same light wood, and a chair padded with flowered material that matched the curtains.

Barbara sat down at the dressing table and began to inspect her face.

"What a wonderful place to squeeze blackheads," she said.

"Barbara, don't! You'll be all blotchy when you go out of here!"

"Oh. I forgot." She turned around on the dressing table stool. "I'd just as soon stay here and pick my face as go out there," she admitted.

"Why?" I was surprised. Barbara hadn't even hinted at such a thing before. I thought she wanted to come to the party.

"They're going to play Post Office." Her eyes grew large with apprehension. "Doris Gregory told me this afternoon. She says they always do at the eighth grade parties."

"What's that?" I felt uneasy, too, although I had never heard of the game. If it included running, I'd be the cow's tail with my knees bent.

"It's a kissing game. Somebody is the postmaster and he stands at the door. Then the one inside says who she wants to kiss and the postmaster calls his name and he comes in, and afterwards its his turn to say who he wants."

"How horrible!" I thought of the boys in my room. There wasn't one I'd want to kiss.

"Well, maybe they won't play it." I tried to reassure her. "Mrs. Chenoworth is right here. I'm sure she wouldn't allow such a thing in her house."

"Maybe you're right." Barbara stood up. "Well, we can't stay here anyway."

She walked out and I tottered along behind her.

The boys were all sitting on one side of the room giggling behind their masks and scuffling with each other. The girls sat on the other side.

"Now that we're all here," said Mrs. Chenoworth gaily,

"we'd better start the games. First we're going to see whether the boys or the girls can carry more beans on a knife."

I breathed a sigh of relief, partly because I figured she had arranged the games beforehand and they wouldn't include Post Office, and partly because in carrying beans on a knife you had to walk slowly.

We lined up, and when she said go, we dipped our knives into a sack of dried beans and tried to get as many as we could. Then we carried them carefully across the room and dumped them into a basket before hurrying back and giving our knives to someone else on our side.

Since I had to walk carefully anyway I didn't lose a single bean from my knife, and when it was time to hurry back I just lifted my skirt a little to take longer steps.

The girls won because the boys were so clumsy and tried to carry too many beans on their knives. When that happened, they had to come back to the sacks and start again.

"I'm afraid those masks are making it difficult for the boys to concentrate." Mrs. Chenoworth looked dotingly at her son. "Suppose we take them off and give our prizes for the best costume?" She went on to say that there would be three prizes, one for the prettiest, one for the funniest and one for the most original. Mr. and Mrs. Chenoworth and Eldon, who couldn't compete since he was the host, would be the judges.

We all lined up, everybody tugging at some part of a costume and trying to look nonchalant. I had to readjust my veil, which had become twisted in the bean game. Then I went to stand by Barbara.

Marian Tilson won the prettiest costume, though I thought Barbara Simmons' Bo Peep was prettier. Marian was in the eighth grade and she came as Miss Liberty. She wore white drapings that I swear must have been a bed sheet, with a red, white and blue ribbon across one shoulder and tied at the opposite side of her waist. Kenny Wardon, also from the eighth grade, won the funniest. He was the horned red devil who had occupied the front seat with Mr. Chenoworth and Eldon. And much to my surprise, I won the prize for the most unique.

"I hear Miss Pope made it, dear," whispered Mrs. Chenoworth as she pinned the winner's ribbon on my chest. "I'm glad skirts like that aren't worn by ladies, but you must congratulate Miss Pope from me for her originality."

"You old bat," I thought to myself, squirming as the pin pricked my skin. "If Miss Edna's right and full skirts are the style, you'll be the first one down there begging her to make you one." Of course, I didn't say it aloud.

"Now, if you don't need me and have everything in hand, I think I'll run downtown for a while. I'll pick up your ice cream on the way back." Mr. Chenoworth didn't wait for his wife to answer. He was out the door before she had a chance.

"Remember, all three kinds," she shrieked after him. "Chocolate, strawberry and vanilla." She turned to us, a fixed little smile on her face. "We don't need him anyway," she told us. "I have a whole list of games for you to play. The next one is—"

"Post Office," interrupted Eldon, coming to stand next to her. "We're going to play Post Office. I talked to the other boys and all of us want to."

"Post Office!" She hesitated. Evidently she knew the game. "Oh, Eldon, no! It's not a nice game. I'm sure some of the mothers—"

He took her arm and led her to a chair before a little desk placed in the corner.

"You sit right here," he ordered. "It's my party, not yours. Now who wants to be postmaster?"

"I will," offered the red devil, who was Kenny. "So far as I'm concerned it's the most fun of the game."

"Eldon, please," pleaded his mother, but he ignored her.

"Who wants to go first?"

"I will," offered Buzz Snider. He was another eighth grade boy whom I hardly knew.

"Go into the guest room then," ordered Eldon. "It's over there, where the girls put their things."

Buzz went inside and shut the door. Immediately he knocked from the inside.

Kenny opened the door and all we could see was darkness. Buzz must have turned out the lights. When Kenny closed the door again there was a wide grin on his face.

"A special delivery letter for Marian Tilson," he announced.

With a flourish of her draperies, Marian got up and managed to avoid the feet of the boys sitting on the sofa. Then she went inside the dark bedroom. She was gone for quite a while, and when the door opened Buzz came out alone.

I felt Barbara's hand reaching for mine and I held it tightly. We both hoped they would limit the game to members of the eighth grade.

For a little while they did, then someone called Eldon Chenoworth. I suppose they almost had to since it was his party. Barbara and I gripped each other tightly, and when the red devil at the door announced, "Marty Burnham. A registered letter for Marty Burnham," I just sat there.

"It's for you, Marty," called Doris Gregory. "Go in and get your letter."

Barbara extracted her fingers from mine, and I made myself stand up. If you think it's easy to do, keeping your knees bent, just try it. Behind me I could hear the tittering of the eighth graders. At least, I told myself, I was stronger than Eldon Chenoworth. If he tried to kiss me I'd just sock him.

Kenny opened the door for me, pushed me in and closed it behind me. Through the shadows I could see a large mass advancing toward me.

"That will do," I said icily. "You may go now."

"But—but—" stammered Eldon.

"I said, go!" This time I almost shouted it, and he went. I know his pride would keep him from telling anyone what had happened.

In a moment Kenny opened the door. I could see his devil's horns sticking around the door jamb.

"Do you have a letter for someone, miss?" he asked, giggling a little.

I thought frantically. Who could I handle?

"Yes," I said sweetly. "Freddy Taylor. I have something for Freddy Taylor."

The door closed and I looked at the bed. There was my blue sweater next to Barbara's on the heap of wraps. I tucked it under my left arm and waited.

Pretty soon Freddy came in, swaggering a little in his tall silk "Lincoln" hat. When Kenny shut the door, I let Freddy have it, just the way we used to do before Mama told me I couldn't fight with boys. I heard him grunt but I didn't wait to see what damage I had done.

"That was short and sweet," said Kenny when I came out. "Must have been a love note."

Everybody laughed. I headed straight for Mrs. Chenoworth, still sitting at her desk. She looked so uncomfortable I felt sorry for her. She didn't know what to do. I walked straight up without bending my knees. I was tired of it, and if people wanted to laugh at my black Mary Janes, they could.

"I'm afraid I have to leave now, Mrs. Chenoworth," I told her sweetly. "I'm supposed to be in bed at nine. Besides I have a little headache."

"So have I," she admitted. "Why don't we both take a head-ache powder? I have one that does wonders for headaches."

"I'd better not," I insisted quickly. "I'd better go right now."

"But Mr. Chenoworth isn't here to drive you. And the party lasts till ten."

"That's why I have to leave so early. Papa hit the roof when he saw that, because my bedtime is nine. Thank you for the party, Mrs. Chenoworth."

When I turned to leave I could see that everyone was staring at me. The eighth graders were smirking and some of the seventh graders looked as though they'd like to come with me.

I stepped outside into the starry night, hoisted my skirt up to my knees and began to run.

Chapter 14

I SAT WITH BARBARA at Sunday school the next day. "What happened after I left the party?" I whispered. "Did you have to kiss somebody?"

"No," she told me thankfully. "Mr. Chenoworth came home just after you left, and was he mad when he saw what was going on! He blamed poor Mrs. Chenoworth, as though she could do anything with that awful Eldon. He opened his presents, then we had our ice cream and cake and Mr. Chenoworth took everybody home early."

"What did he get?" I asked, wondering that Mama had wrapped up.

"Handkerchiefs mostly." She giggled. "Every one of us girls gave him handkerchiefs. But what else could you give a boy? There were at least two in every box. He'll have enough handkerchiefs to last the rest of his life. Of course, the boys gave different things, like jackknives and balls and junk."

I was pleased with Mama. She'd known just what to buy! When I'd come running home the night before, she and Papa had been upset and full of questions. Why had I left the party early? If I had a headache why hadn't Mr. Chenoworth driven me home? And so on. I avoided all their questions because there are some things that you have to protect your family from. I didn't want to tell them about the Post Office game and how I'd socked Freddy Taylor. I just said I had a headache and Mr. Chenoworth had already gone for the ice cream. I didn't tell them that I had run all the way.

"She is flushed." Mama had worried, feeling my hot cheeks. "And I think she may have a little fever, too. I'll just give her some Castoria and she can go right to bed."

"I knew she was too young to be out so late. You should have called me, or had Mrs. Chenoworth call, Marty. I'd have come after you." Papa sounded only relieved that I was home. I wondered how much he guessed. Papa was pretty smart.

When I was fine in the morning, they decided it was just a passing thing and I could go to Sunday school as usual.

"Another thing happened after you'd gone," whispered Barbara. "Freddy Taylor had a bad nose bleed. It took a long while for Mrs. Chenoworth to get it stopped. His nose looked sort of swollen, too. He said he'd run into the door."

"Girls," said the Sunday school teacher, "there's been quite enough whispering. Kindly pay attention to the lessons."

I wondered if I'd dare tell Barbara that Freddy had run into my fist, not a door. Then I decided I wouldn't. Like Eldon, Freddy would keep my secret.

As soon as I got home and changed my clothes I went out to the fence. Antoinette was waiting for me, and it was safe to tell her everything that happened.

"Oh, I wish I could see your dress and veil," she said wistfully when I told her about Miss Edna's making them.

"Climb your ladder and come over the wall, and I'll show them to you," I coaxed.

"I can't—I just can't leave Rebecca," she explained patiently. "Go on about the party."

"Well, you wouldn't have liked this one." After I had told her all about it, she agreed.

"You did exactly the right thing," she said. "I wonder what a boy looks like. Up close, I mean."

I couldn't believe the things she had to learn, shut up in that prison for years. If only she'd let me tell Papa! Some way or the other I had to find a way to get her out. It was hard because we'd talked about it before and she wouldn't leave Miss Rebecca. I guess I understood. After all, she was her mother. They'd *both* have to leave.

There was one other person I told about the party and that was Miss Edna. She'd made me promise to give her a full report so that afternoon I went to her house.

She was busy at her sewing machine, but she stopped the minute I arrived.

"I usually don't sew on the Lord's Day," she told me. "But I'd put Mrs. Forbes off, and when she comes for a fitting I want her dress basted together."

She got a plate of cookies, two glasses of milk, and we sat down at the kitchen table.

"Now tell me about your dress. Did people like it?"

"I won a prize. I want you to have it." I pulled out the white ribbon with the letters "most original" written in red crayon.

"Most original!" She laughed. "I just copied a picture from an *Advance* design book. They'll all be wearing that style by fall, you mark my word. Well, what about the party? Did you play games?"

Before I knew it, I was telling Miss Edna all about Post Office and what I'd done to Eldon and Freddy when it was my turn, and how I'd run all the way home.

"Good for you," she approved. "The other girls should have done the same thing."

"Did they play Post Office when you were a little girl and went to parties?" I asked.

"I never went to a party." Her tone was very matter of fact. "I wasn't asked. I don't know what the others did because I didn't have any friends to talk with. I was an outsider. I went to school and got good grades because I studied. But I never had a friend in school. People were afraid to be my friend. The others would have laughed at them."

"Oh, Miss Edna," I felt the tears coming and I couldn't stop them. They began sliding down my cheeks.

"Now, now," she said, patting my hand. "It wasn't so bad. I always had a home to come to, and my grandparents loved me. My grandmother taught me to sew, and Grandpa bought me a big doll. It was expensive, more than he could afford probably. So when I came home I'd make dresses and hats for her. I didn't have patterns, but I learned to look at pictures and I tried to make the dresses like the pictures. As you see, it was good training. I didn't need friends. I had my doll, Henrietta."

"You've got me now," I reminded her.

"Bless you, child. So I have. And nowadays I have lots of people who claim to be my friend so that I'll design their clothes! But someday…someday…"

"Someday what?" I demanded.

"I'll tell you when the time comes," she promised. "You'll be the first to know because you are my first friend."

The following week was the last before the summer vacation, so we didn't have much to do. The teachers had probably already made up their minds what grades to give us, and we didn't do much studying. On Friday, we picked up our report cards. I got A's in everything except arithmetic. I barely passed in that. My parents didn't say as much as they might have about that because everyone was concentrating on the total eclipse, which would happen the next day.

"Now remember, Marty," said Mama for the umpteenth time. "You mustn't look at the sun while the eclipse is going on except through smoked glass, and then only for less than a second."

She had broken the chimney of an oil lamp into big pieces and was holding the pieces over the flame of the lamp so that they would get smoky black.

"What would happen if I did?"

"You'd go blind," she told me flatly.

"I'll stay in my room then, with the shades down."

"They claim this will be safe," she argued. "It's all in the paper. There won't be another eclipse of the sun until 1979."

"We'll all be dead by that time."

"Your Papa and I will, but you might not be. Just make sure you protect your eyes so you can see it. And don't look very long at a time."

The way Mama made us watch the eclipse I didn't get much out of it. She and Papa and I went out in the front yard, carrying our pieces of smoked lamp chimney. She'd smoked them so black you could hardly see through them, and we had to stand with our back to the sun. It was a bright blue day, all sparkly and warm.

"Now," Mama would cry, and we'd all whirl around with the blackened glass in front of our eyes. Almost before we got focused, she'd shriek, "Turn around!"

In these short glimpses I could see the shadow of the moon creep across the sun. It moved very fast and before long it was perfectly dark. It was the darkest dark I'd ever seen and it felt like night. There was even a breeze like the wind that comes up at night. All the stars were out.

"Now," cried Mama, and when we turned there was

nothing there to see. "Back," she called, and Papa and Mama and I revolved again.

"Now it will retreat," declared Mama. "It will go back in the same order that it came. Turn now."

But I'd had enough. An eclipse of the sun was boring, I decided. I went back to the house.

"Don't look out the window," Mama called after me. I didn't even want to. As I turned on the light I wondered how many people in King Arthur's court went blind from looking at the eclipse. That's one of the things Mr. Twain didn't tell about when he wrote *The Connecticut Yankee*.

It was the worst summer vacation I ever spent. Because so many men were gone, the women and children had to harvest the fruit. We'd be slackers if we didn't, so I gritted my teeth and went every day to the fields.

First there were strawberries. You had to crawl along and part the leaves to find them because they weren't always on the top. There was a special way of picking them, too. You couldn't put in clods of dirt, and the little berries had to go in the bottom, with the big juicy ones one top.

They said people in Germany were starving, and sometimes I wished we could turn some of them loose in those strawberry fields that seemed to go on and on. Then I would remember Glen French and I was glad they didn't have our strawberries and were hungry. At least Andy wasn't hungry. We'd heard from him by this time, and he was perfectly fine except for bruises and a few cuts. He said he didn't mind them because they gave him time to recover. If I knew Andy, he'd make those bruises last as long as possible.

After strawberries there were raspberries. They weren't so bad because you could stand up and sometimes squat down and rest while you pretended to be looking for berries underneath. But the overseers were there, too, pointing out berries you had missed. I made one dollar a day there, the same as I had with the strawberries. After that there were cherries, dark Lamberts and Bings and pale Royal Annes. Papa wouldn't let me pick cherries because you had to climb a ladder, but it didn't matter. The second crop of peas was coming on and I picked them.

When I got home the kitchen would be blazing hot because Mama would have been canning all day. You can't can vegetables or fruit without fire and our wood stove burned all day long, even in the hottest weather, but there were always long rows of glass jars filled with food for next winter. Then came the tomatoes and late beans, and after that the hops and prunes, which we picked up off the ground to help save the world for democracy and got stung by yellow jackets while we were doing it.

It was the most miserable summer I ever spent. I even envied Antoinette for being locked up behind her wall so she didn't have to harvest fruit. She said she envied me, but I still couldn't talk her into leaving. Not without Miss Rebecca, and Miss Rebecca was too scared of her mother to budge an inch.

When the last prune was picked, they opened school again, and then I was an eighth grader, the top class in the school. It's funny, but I didn't feel any different, and when I asked them, neither did Fay or Barbara.

We still had to keep on saving the world for democracy, buying thrift stamps and knitting washcloths and saving foil, but now we had to collect pieces of rubber, too, worn out tires mostly.

Henry Riggs filled up our woodshed—luckily we didn't have to save wood—and it was fun to watch. He always started at the back and made neat rows up to the ceiling, then a second row right next to that clear out to the door. We never had to buy any wood, anymore than we did manure for the garden. Some client of Papa's always paid his bill that way.

Every day Papa read about something called the Spanish Influenza in the paper, and every day he and Mama worried about it. When I asked Antoinette if Mrs. Hutchinson was worried she said she didn't know. They didn't take the paper and the first she'd heard about it was when I told her.

"It's getting closer and closer," said Mama one night at supper. "Maybe it won't come here. We're so out of the way. It seems to hit worse in the cities."

"Maybe," said Papa. "But I doubt it. It seems to be in the air."

Pretty soon there were cases in Portland and we knew we were in for it. The paper said people were dying from it by the thousands. Since it was new, the doctors didn't know what to do for it. They were treating it like La Grippe. Quinine and liquids, stay in bed and get the fever down.

I don't know who got it first, but overnight there were a dozen cases of Spanish Influenza in Maple Glen. Mayor Kirkpatrick ordered all schools closed and all public meetings were abolished. It kept right on. Churches were closed, too, though some people thought that was going against God. Then some of the stores began to close, but not the grocery store or drugstore. They had to stay open, but the clerks wore white cloths tied around their mouths and noses so they wouldn't breathe the same air as the customers. Ed Brown, who ran Mrs. Hutchinson's hardware store, came down with it, so she took charge. She went every day, not just Tuesdays and Fridays. I figured she was safe. She was too mean for any bug to dare bite her.

One morning when I woke up I didn't feel very well. I threw up on the way to the bathroom and when Mama took one look at me she told Papa to call Dr. McCallum.

"It's the flu," he said. "Lots of liquids when she can keep them down and give her quinine till her head rings."

How I hated that. They kept giving you quinine almost every hour and pretty soon it sounded as if bells were ringing inside your head.

"Keep her warm, too," said Dr. McCallum. "We've got to get that fever down. At least one more quilt on the bed."

I was so hot then I didn't see how being hotter would help, but I was too sick to say so.

Mama ran for the extra quilt and Papa hurried to the drug store for more quinine. The doctor left some kind of medicine, a pink powder, that was dissolved in hot water. Mama put it in a tin cup with a spout to drink from, and when Papa came back they gave me more quinine.

I don't remember how long I was sick, but Dr. McCallum said I had a light case. I was lucky. It seemed to be hardest on children and old people.

Pretty soon they let me come downstairs and sit in the Morris chair, with a blanket over me, and things began to look better. I asked Mama how many people had influenza.

"Too many," she said sadly. "There are three or four funerals a day. We can just thank God you came through it, Marty."

But it was boring sitting in the Morris chair. I cut out paper doll families from an old Montgomery Ward catalog until I thought I'd go crazy. Then I thought about Antoinette and hoped Mrs. Hutchinson had told her I'd been sick. She must have wondered when I wasn't at the wall on Sunday.

"Tomorrow," said Mama, "I think we'll let you get up and walk around the house. You've made a remarkable recovery. But you must take it easy."

The next day I got up, all right, but I didn't take it very easy. Mama had come down with the Spanish Influenza.

Chapter 15

MAMA WAS AWFULLY SICK, sicker than I had been. There were no nurses to be had, so Papa stayed home to take care of her.

"What if you should get it, too?" I worried.

"I won't get it," he told me confidently. "I'm a tough old goat." And strangely enough he didn't.

Dr. McCallum came again and prescribed the same things he had for me.

"Someday we'll have medicines to fight such things," he said. "But we don't now. We just have to do the best we can."

Aunt Gertrude came to the front door with a jar of chicken broth for Mama and a meat loaf for Papa and me. She wouldn't come inside.

"We have to take precautions these days," she told us. "I worry so about Horace working at the post office every day and having to face all those people. I tell him to stand well back and wash his hands after he's handled any money. Tell Bea I hope she feels better soon, and oh yes, I called Mama on the telephone and told her not to come to town. It's better to be warned, you know."

As I watched her go sailing down the front walk, grasping her hat to straighten it out in the wind, I almost hated my Aunt Gertrude.

The next day Grandma arrived. I was stirring some of Doc McCallum's pink fever powder in hot water to dissolve it, and Papa was in Mama's room getting her to swallow another quinine capsule when the front door opened.

"Where's Beatrice?" demanded Grandma loudly. "And what's all this about the La Grippe?"

Papa hurried to the bedroom door.

"You'd better not come in, Martha," he advised. "It's very contagious."

"Fiddle-dee-dee," said Grandma scornfully. "I didn't take the plague when we crossed the plains, did I? And all around me people in other wagons were dropping off like flies."

I stopped stirring and came out of the kitchen to watch. The minute Mama had heard Grandma's voice, she raised up from the pillow.

"Mama, you get out of here," she ordered, and though her voice was weak, you could tell she meant it. "Gertrude had no business calling you."

"And who's going to nurse you, I should like to know?"

"I am," said Papa. "I've had practice. Look at Marty, up and around and feeling fine."

"I won't have you in here." Mama began to cry. "This is hardest on old people and children. Stay out of this room, Mama."

"And why should I, when it's my plain duty to be here?" asked Grandma.

"Because you're my mother and I love you," said Mama.

Grandma got a funny expression on her face, and for a minute she didn't say anything.

"Very well," she agreed. "I'll stay out of your room, but I won't stay out of your kitchen. Sam can't do everything. And

Martha here has had the La Grippe so she won't get it again. They can fetch and carry, but I'll give the orders."

"You can have Marty's bed." Papa sounded grateful.

He wasn't much of a cook and Grandma was.

"Oh, no." She smiled a little wickedly. "I'll sleep at Gertrude's. It's the least she can do. And speaking of sleep, as soon as you help Jim unload the buggy, Sam, you march upstairs and catch yourself forty winks. You look like you need it."

Grandma went to the kitchen, where we could hear her snorting about the dirty dishes we hadn't had time to wash and I went outside with Papa.

Grandpa was standing at the front of the buckboard patting Buford's nose. Buford was his regular buggy horse, although there were six or eight others in the farm corral. Buford was blind, but everybody was so good to him I don't think he cared. He always had the best stall, the first scoop of oats, and the only trip he ever made was from Grandpa's farm to Maple Glen. I think he could tell by the smells just where he was for he kept turning his head as though he might be sniffing at things.

Grandpa reached in his overcoat pocket and brought out two pieces of horehound candy. He gave the first one to Buford and the second to me.

"How is she?" he asked Papa. "Bad as Gertrude made out?"

"She's pretty bad," said Papa.

"Martha'll see to it," said Grandpa confidently.

"Bea won't let her in the same room."

"Won't matter," said Grandpa. "Everything'll be fine now. Soon as I finished the milking she had me out, ready to leave. Even packed most of the buckboard herself. I don't know what all's there, but you can believe she thought of everything."

"I'll help you carry it in," said Papa, reaching for a knobby gunny sack on the floor. The minute he did, there was a great squawking of chickens.

"A couple of old hens and a rooster," explained Grandpa. "For broth."

"We have chickens," Papa told him stiffly.

"I know. But Martha picked these out especially for broth. Better turn them loose in your barnyard. She'll find them again."

By that time I had finished picking all the flakes of pipe tobacco off the horehound and put it in my mouth. Grandpa carried his loose pipe tobacco in the same pocket, and while Buford didn't mind, I didn't like tobacco.

There was a sack of onions, a flat iron, some red flannel and some other stuff in sacks that I couldn't identify. Then he unloaded Grandma's valise last of all.

"She says she's not going to sleep here." Papa had returned from letting the chickens loose in the barnyard by that time. "Says she's going to sleep at Gertrude's."

I could see Grandpa's fine teeth shining through his beard as he smiled.

"Then that's what she'll do," he said. "Martha was madder than a setting hen off her nest when Gertrude telephoned and said she hadn't seen Beatrice because she didn't want germs in her house. Germs! Whoever saw a germ anyway? So Martha will spend her days here and carry some of those germs back to Gertrude's house every night. She didn't tell me, but that's what she aims to do."

He and Papa grinned at each other.

"You want to come in, Jim?" asked Papa.

"Think Beatrice will see me?"

Papa shook his head.

"Then there's no need," said Grandpa. "Just tell her that I

wish her well. I'll take Martha's valise down to Gertrude's and tell her to expect her ma tonight. I got a bit of trading in town and then I'll head home. Stock to take care of."

He gave Buford and me each another piece of horehound, then drove off. As soon as he was gone I threw mine in the bushes. It wasn't worth picking off the tobacco.

When I got back to the kitchen, Grandma had the dishes all done and was cutting hunks of meat, which she put in a jar with a screw lid.

"I'm making beef tea," she announced. "Nothing so nourishing as beef tea. There's some that don't use salt, but I always add a little when it's done. Makes it go down easier."

She popped the sealed jar of meat into a kettle filled with water and set it on the hottest part of the stove.

"Shouldn't you have added a little water to the meat, Grandma?" I asked timidly. How could anyone make tea without water?

"Gracious, no!" She glared at me as though I'd asked if the moon was really made of green cheese. "The water's in the meat. It'll all cook out and then you'll have straight juice. Add water indeed!"

I watched, fascinated, and sure enough a little juice began to gather in the jar with the boiling meat.

Papa came into the kitchen.

"She finally fell asleep," he said. "She had a coughing spell that kept her awake."

"I've got ears," said Grandma. "And I don't like the sound of it neither, so I'm getting ready. When she wakes up, I'll have a nice hot onion plaster for her chest. I'll have to trust you to put it on, though, Sam, since I'm not allowed in her room. Though why someone who lived through the plague shouldn't live through this Spanish thingamajig, I don't know."

There was a big pot of sliced onions simmering on the back of the stove. I couldn't help being pleased that Grandma wasn't serving them for supper. I hated cooked onions.

"But Dr. McCallum didn't say—"

"I'm in charge now," said Grandma flatly. "You leave it to me. You go catch those forty winks I told you to. You're about to drop on your feet. Me and Martha can manage."

Papa didn't argue, so I guess he really was tired. We heard the bed springs squeak once when he got in, then he began to snore.

About that time we heard Mama moving around in her room and coughing.

"I guess you'll have to do it, Martha," said Grandma. "She won't let me in and the onions are ready. Now, I'll tell you just what to do."

When Mama saw me coming with the pot of cooked onions and the piece of red flannel, she sighed.

"An onion poultice! I knew she'd do it. I just knew it."

"Does it hurt?" I asked anxiously.

"No. I was never too sure that poultices did much good, but we'll have to go through with it, you and I, or she'll come marching in here and get the Spanish Influenza."

She unbuttoned the front of her nightgown, exposing her chest.

"Get a handful of onions and spread it as thick as you can," she ordered weakly. "From my throat, almost to my stomach. You'll have to use all the onions or she'll send you back. Then cover it with the flannel and tuck it in."

The onions were warm and slimy to the touch, but I did as Mama told me.

"How does it feel?" I asked when I was finished.

"Like when I was a child." She smiled almost wistfully.

"The onion plasters I've had in my lifetime, though mustard is worse."

The funny thing was we didn't hear her cough after that. Maybe she went back to sleep.

The beef tea was done, Grandma announced. Somehow she managed to get the sealed jar from the kettle of boiling water without burning herself. It was a quarter full of dark brown liquid, while the meat was almost white.

"We'll just throw the meat away," she told me. "It's not even fit for the dog. The nourishment is boiled out."

Mama was still asleep and Grandma said not to wake her even if it was time for another capsule of quinine.

"Sleep's better," she declared. "And don't you forget it, Martha Morgan Burnham!"

Papa woke up after a couple of hours and came downstairs, feeling very guilty for deserting us.

"You did no such thing," Grandma told him. "Now if Beatrice is awake you better give her another of those quinine pills Doc McCallum sets such store by. And change the onion plaster on her chest. I got more onions cooked and ready to go. After that she can have a cup of beef tea and we'll eat our own supper."

To my surprise, but not Grandma's, the onion poultice on Mama's chest had changed color. It was now a darkish green, almost black.

"See that!" she cried. "P'ison. I knew there was p'ison in her chest and it has to come out. How'd she take to the tea?"

"She said it was good," Papa admitted. "But she thought she'd have another little nap."

"Good!" Grandma whisked off her apron and took one of the chairs at the kitchen table she had set for three. There were pork chops and cream gravy to spread over the mashed potatoes, string beans that she had canned herself—"though

I wouldn't trust nobody else's"—beets, homemade bread she had brought from the farm and quince preserves.

"You'll have to make bread do for dessert," she told us. "I haven't had time to do anything else, but tomorrow'll be better."

It was the best meal I'd eaten since Mama got sick.

Grandma and I did the dishes and she set another pot of beef tea to simmering on the back of the stove. Mama was sleeping peacefully.

"I done all I can for today," she admitted. "I guess I'll head on to Gertrude's now."

"I'll get the flivver and drive you," offered Papa. "You must be worn out. And I don't know how we can ever thank you."

"Why should you thank me?" she demanded, glaring. "But I would take kindly to a ride to Gertrude's. My corns is killing me. My, I can hardly wait to see her face when I walk in breathing out all them germs."

Grandma stayed a week, and by that time Mama was up and around the house. She got tired easily, but that was to be expected, and Grandma said she'd perk up when she got enough solid food inside of her. Anybody would be weak living on beef tea and chicken soup.

Grandpa came after her in the buckboard and before she climbed in she did a strange thing. She patted me on the shoulder.

"You're a good girl, Martha Morgan Burnham," she told me. "And I'm right glad they named you after me."

Strangest of all, I was too.

Chapter 16

THE FLU—BY NOW EVERYBODY had stopped using the word "Spanish"—was universal. We read that there were two hundred twenty-three thousand cases in the army and we worried about Andy, so far from home. I wished Grandma could go over there with her beef tea and onion poultices. She'd fix them up in a hurry.

Some people said the flu was carried by the Germans, who had shot flu germs from their guns. But Papa said that couldn't be true because the Germans had it, too, and they wouldn't want to infect their own people. Luckily it had about run its course in Maple Glen. People were even talking about reopening churches and schools, and a lot of stores were open.

"Hutchinson's Hardware is closed," said Papa one evening when he came home for supper. "I stopped by for some nails and Nick Peters told me Ed Brown's been out for a week. The old lady tried running it herself, but every day must have been too much for her. She hung out a 'Closed' sign last Monday."

"Well, at least she isn't exposed to flu germs behind her high wall," I said.

"Unless she brought the germs home with her," said Mama. "Sam, do you think I—"

"No," he said quickly. "If she wants help, she'll ask for it."

When we finished supper. Mama went to the kitchen and came back with a cake that had thirteen blue and white candles blazing on it.

"Happy birthday, Marty," she said, putting it in front of me.

It had been such a crazy mixed-up year that I'd even forgotten it was my birthday. I just sat there staring at the candles.

"I'm sorry it can't be a party," she said. "But with all the flu we thought we couldn't take a chance."

I blew out the candles, but before I cut the cake there were presents. Papa gave me a twenty-five dollar Liberty Bond and Mama had two books for me, *Treasure Island* and *Betty Wales.*

"I'm afraid that this is mostly trash," she said as I unwrapped the second book. "But I notice you bring back trash sometimes from the library."

They also gave me a new pair of bedroom slippers and a pink bathrobe to match.

"Oh thank you! Thank you!" It was especially nice they had remembered my birthday when I had forgotten. I told myself I must be growing up. I'd never forgotten a birthday before.

Just then there was a knock on the door, and when Papa opened it it was Miss Edna.

"I won't stay," she apologized. "And I'm sorry I caught you at mealtime. I just wanted to leave a little token for Marty's birthday."

"How did you know?" I asked, and I was glad to see that Papa was pulling up a chair at the table.

"You told me, once. A long time ago. You've probably forgotten, but I put a ring around my calendar so I wouldn't," she confessed.

"You're just in time for birthday cake," said Mama. "Let Sam take your coat and then sit down next to Marty."

It took a little while to persuade her, but she finally did, depositing a fat squashy bundle in my lap at the same time. When I tore off the wrappings there was a pillow covered in patchwork, with tiny embroidered flowers in the largest pieces.

"It's just scraps from dressmaking," she apologized to Mama. "But Marty took a fancy to them, so I worked it up for her. I didn't realize when I first asked her to come to see me that she was too old for dolls."

"I'm not sure that she is," Mama said dryly. She didn't mention my dollhouse, for which I was very grateful. "The pillow is lovely and what workmanship! It's a thing of art she can keep forever."

"Here's the piece of red velvet I liked," I exclaimed. "Right in the middle. See, Mama?"

"It's beautiful," agreed Mama, stroking it gently.

Miss Edna had been very uncomfortable at first, but as we praised her pillow she seemed to relax and the smile that changed her whole face appeared.

I sliced the cake and Mama poured cups of hot tea.

"That tea really warms you up," Miss Edna told Mama. "The wind is fierce tonight and it's raining cats and dogs."

"And you came out in it," said Mama clucking her tongue. "Just to bring Marty a present."

I hadn't noticed it before—we were snug and warm at the table before the fireplace—but the rain was pounding at the windows and occasionally the wind blew down the chimney, making the fire flame and sputter.

It was then that there was the second knock on the door. Papa opened it and at first it was so dark I couldn't see anyone there.

"Come in, come in," urged Papa. "Marty, this must be another friend to see you."

A girl stepped inside the door and stood shivering under a thin, dripping shawl. She was a lot smaller than I was, with a pinched face nearly blue with the cold. Her hair was pulled tightly back into a single braid and below the shawl the folds of a long gray calico dress clung and hung tightly to her ankles. I had never seen her before, but I knew her at once.

"Antoinette!"

"Marty," she whispered.

"Mama, Papa, Miss Edna," I said hurriedly, taking the sodden shawl from her thin shoulders. "This is Antoinette. She's lived next door for ten years. She's Miss Rebecca's daughter."

"Rebecca Hutchinson!" gasped Miss Edna.

"Gracious me!" Mama stood up, letting her napkin fall to the floor. "Marty run upstairs and get your warmest nightgown and robe and bring that pair of bedroom slippers you just outgrew. I want bath towels, too. We've got to get her hair dry before she catches her death of cold."

Apparently only Papa and Miss Edna had heard what I said.

"Miss Rebecca's daughter," repeated Papa. "And you've lived next door all that time?"

"All my life," Antoinette mumbled, and Papa's face took on that stern look that he uses in court.

"I don't see how—" he began, but Mama interrupted him.

"There's time for that later. Right now we've got to get her warm and dry."

"No, ma'am," objected Antoinette. "I've got to go back. Rebecca's sick. She's awful sick. And Mrs. Hutchinson's sick, too. She came down with it first. But now she must be better because she just lies there, all white and funny-looking. Rebecca can't wait on her any more because she's sick herself. She told me I'd have to get help. The only place I could think of was Marty's."

"I'll go right over," said Papa, reaching for the rubber coat he wore in the barnyard on rainy days.

"I'm going with you," said Mama. "I've had the flu so I won't get it again. If you don't mind staying with the girls, Edna?"

"Of course not," she agreed quickly, taking the flannel nightgown from me and holding it before the fire to get it warm. "You run along. And if there's anything I can do for Rebecca—"

"We'll see," promised Mama as she and Papa stepped out into the rainy night.

"Now," said Miss Edna cheerfully. "Off with your clothes, my dear. All of them. Just drop them on the hearth and I'll take care of them later."

Antoinette did as she was told, and I was even more amazed to see how scrawny she looked without any clothes. Miss Edna slipped the gown over her head and helped her on with the bathrobe. Although it was tight for me, it was miles too big for her. Miss Edna had to roll up the sleeves and it trailed on the floor. The slippers, too, were much too large but Miss Edna made her put them on anyway. Then she unbraided Antoinette's hair and rubbed it briskly with a towel. It had looked black when it was wet, but as it dried it turned out to be brown. All the time Miss Edna was dressing her, she talked.

"Where is your father, dear? Does he ever come to see you?"

"He can't," explained Antoinette. "Marty laughed when I told her, but I never had a father."

"And you've never been outside the wall?" said Miss Edna, rubbing at Antoinette's hair.

"Once," Antoinette hung her head. "I slipped out one day when Marty wasn't here and had left Caesar. I heard him crying, so I came to get him. But Rebecca says I mustn't ever do that again. She says I've got to hide when anyone's around so no one will know I'm there. If I don't, Mrs. Hutchinson will send me to the orphanage."

"Fiddle-dee-dee," said Miss Edna, and I could tell she was very angry. "How did you know about Marty? Did she climb over the wall? It's what I would have done at your age."

So we told her the whole story, about Antoinette knocking on the wall and me answering. We told her how we could only talk on Sundays, because then both Mrs. Hutchinson and Miss Rebecca were in church.

"They're some Christians, aren't they?" said Miss Edna sarcastically, but Antoinette took her seriously.

"Oh yes, every evening Mrs. Hutchinson reads aloud from the Bible. And we listen. She says Rebecca has sinned and I'm the fruit of that sin. That's why she always calls me Sinette. That means little sin."

"Barbaric!" Miss Edna snorted.

"It could be worse," I reminded her. "It was worse what they did to Hester Prynne. She always had to wear a big A sewed on the front of her dress."

"Who's Hester Prynne?" demanded Miss Edna finally.

"She's a lady in a book called *The Scarlet Letter*. And it's what they used to do to women who were…were…"

"Adulteresses," finished Miss Edna for me, when I couldn't make myself say the word.

"But that happened a long time ago—a hundred years maybe," I added quickly. "They don't do that anymore."

"Not quite," admitted Miss Edna, gently pushing Antoinette

into a chair before the fireplace. "But what they do today is talk, and that's just as bad. Because wherever you go you know what people are thinking."

I don't believe that Antoinette was even listening. Evidently she was tired, for as soon as she sat down she closed her eyes.

At that moment Mama opened the front door in a great burst of wet wind.

"Mrs. Hutchinson is dead," she said softly. "Sam is staying until the undertaker gets there. Rebecca is pretty sick, but not too sick to worry about her daughter. I told her we'd keep her here, but I had to promise no one else would see her. Mrs. Barndecker has had the flu so she agreed to come over and take care of Rebecca till she's well."

"The child will be safer at my house than she would be here," said Miss Edna thoughtfully. "People aren't having sewing done, with all the flu going around. But I don't know why Rebecca can't face up to things."

"Not everyone's as brave as you are, Edna," Mama told her gently. "Rebecca's as timid as a—a rabbit. She cares what people say. Here, I had to clean out Antoinette's things so Mrs. Barndecker wouldn't see them. People say she's something of a snoop."

Antoinette's "things" consisted of another dress like the one she was wearing. It was gray and white calico with long sleeves and a high neck, two flannel nightgowns made in the same style, a suit of one-piece underwear, a brush and comb and a pair of high-topped black lace shoes that had seen better days. She didn't even have a coat.

"Hmph!" said Miss Edna scornfully. She turned the dress wrong side out and inspected the stitching. "All handmade, even to the sideseams, and a creditable job, too."

"I'm sure Rebecca made them," said Mama gently. "Mrs. Hutchinson wouldn't have turned a hand for the child."

"Why don't you put her to bed for tonight," suggested Miss Edna thoughtfully. "The storm's sure to blow itself out. I'll come and fetch her tomorrow after its dark and there's nobody on the streets to speak of."

"If you're sure," said Mama doubtfully.

"I'm sure. And I'll just take these wet things along and dry them out, too. I'll hang them back of the kitchen stove. Even if I have a customer she won't go in there."

"That might be safest if we're to keep Rebecca's secret," agreed Mama. "Look at the poor little thing. Fast asleep. As soon as Sam comes home I'll have him carry her up to bed."

"I'll do it now," volunteered Miss Edna. "Doing for myself all these years has made me strong as an ox. Outside as well as in."

Chapter 17

I DON'T KNOW WHO WENT to Mrs. Hutchinson's funeral except Papa and Ed Brown. Papa had to go because he was Mrs. Hutchinson's lawyer. Mama wouldn't because she said Mrs. Hutchinson was a mean old woman and she'd feel like a hypocrite if she went. Miss Rebecca was too sick to go, and of course Antoinette couldn't, even though she was Mrs. Hutchinson's granddaughter. Anyway, she was buried next to her husband beneath that towering monument in the Pioneer Cemetery. I thought of the moss that would grow on the lion on top and wondered if Miss Rebecca would still clean it off.

Papa told Mama and me that Miss Rebecca was a very wealthy woman now, what with all the money in the bank and the house and the hardware store. She could move away from Maple Glen and no one would know about her and Antoinette. He had been surprised when she refused.

"But this is my home," she had told him. "I know the people. If I went away I wouldn't know a single solitary soul. I wouldn't even know where the grocery store was. It would be too frightening."

"You aren't intending to live inside these walls, are you? And spend the rest of your life here?" Papa had asked frowning.

"Maybe when Antoinette is older I can go," she had admitted. "Maybe she'll grow up brave and strong and won't be afraid. Then we'll both go."

"She won't grow up strong inside a wall," he had said. But Miss Rebecca had only closed her mouth tightly and begun to cry, so he'd let the subject drop.

Antoinette was having a lovely time at Miss Edna's. They'd even driven to Salem and back once, with Antoinette covered with empty cardboard boxes on the floor until they got out of town. Miss Edna had bought her two pairs of shoes, one for everyday and a pair of patent leather Mary Janes for dress-up. I couldn't see much use for the Mary Janes since she couldn't go out. But they made her happy. Miss Edna had taken her to a barber and had her stringy braid cut off and her hair cut into one of those new-fangled bobs that were in all the fashion magazines. Bobbed hair hadn't hit Maple Glen yet, but I wished it would.

Mama had given her my outgrown dresses and Miss Edna cut them down and restyled them so they fit Antoinette. I couldn't believe it when I saw them. They looked better on her than they ever had on me. About the only thing that bothered Antoinette was that she couldn't see her mother because Mrs. Barndecker was still there. So every day I carried messages back and forth between them.

One morning I was at the Hutchinsons'—it must have been a Saturday because there was no school, or maybe it was a special holiday or something—when all the church bells began to ring at once. Maple Glen has five churches, so they made a lot of noise. Then the bell on the fire truck joined them, and there were all sorts of whistles blowing and lots of shouting on the streets.

"What in the world is it?" asked Mrs. Barndecker nervously. "Maybe it's the end of the world."

"I doubt it," I told her, "but I'll run out and see."

When I got outside I could hear people yelling, "It's all over! The war is over! Kaiser Bill has bit the dust!"

I went back just long enough to tell Mrs. Barndecker and Miss Rebecca, then I went back outside. People were singing and shouting and jumping up and down like fleas. I wanted to make noise, too, so I ran back home to tell Mama and got my violin. I paraded up and down the block playing *Over There* and *It's a Long Way to Tipperary* and *Mademoiselle from Armentières* and every other war song I could think of. I didn't often play my violin except in recitals and when I had to practice, so you could see how excited I was.

The Hershys came out on their porch and smiled and waved at me, and the Petersons came out, too, though they didn't make any unladylike noises. They just stood there and clapped their hands.

Later, the newspapers said the Armistice had been signed on the eleventh hour of the eleventh day of the eleventh month. I had a funny thought that it was too bad it couldn't have been the eleventh year of the century, too, but the war hadn't even started in 1911, so that didn't make any sense.

That afternoon I went to Miss Edna's. Miss Rebecca hadn't been able to give me a message because Mrs. Barndecker stuck like a burr that morning. But I could tell them that Miss Rebecca was sitting in a chair while her bed was being changed, which was the first time she'd done that.

Then I saw that Antoinette's face looked woebegone and her under lip was trembling.

"Does that mean you'll be leaving soon, Aunt Edna?" she asked. "You said you were only going to stay till the war was over."

"Very soon now." Miss Edna smiled at her, but there was a determined tilt to her chin. "I was only waiting for the end of the war. People don't buy new dresses much during a war."

"Where are you going?" I asked. Once before Miss Edna had started to tell me something like that, but she'd stopped before she finished.

"To St. Louis," said Miss Edna promptly. I was pretty impressed. It was a long way off, and nobody I knew had ever been there. "Mrs. Kingery from St. Louis was visiting her cousin Mrs. Forbes in Salem. That was before the war, of course. I made her a dress and talked her out of rose satin for gray silk. She was a large woman, you see, and the rose would have made her look like a barn. She was so pleased with the dress when I finished that she begged me to move to St. Louis. She said all her friends would come to me and I was wasting my talents on Maple Glen."

"So you decided to go?"

Miss Edna nodded, "I'm forty-five years old and I've hated nearly every minute I spent in this town. I want to go where no one has ever heard of Edna Pope." She looked at the ceiling and a kind of dreamy expression came over her face. "I'm even going to change my name to Edwina. Edna is so plain."

"Edwina," I repeated stupidly. "Dresses made by Edwina Pope."

"Gowns," she corrected me. "Gowns by Edwina. Doesn't that have a nice sound to it?"

"Maybe Mrs. Whatever-it-is has changed her mind," I suggested for Antoinette's sake. Tears were running down her face. "Or maybe she's moved away."

"I wrote to her," said Miss Edna in a pleased voice. "And she wrote right back. She said she was delighted and wanted me to do a whole spring wardrobe for her. Besides that she's got several ladies lined up for the modiste—that's what I'll be called, not just a plain dressmaker—" She broke off suddenly as she noticed the tears on Antoinette's face. "Don't cry, honey," she said soothingly. "I'll write you every week."

We expected a big change now the war was over, but I didn't see any. Our soldiers had to stay in France or Germany, except those who were very sick or injured. They were sent to hospitals here and the ladies in the Red Cross left off knitting socks and helmets and began on afghans. These were made of bright-colored squares, each six inches across. The squares were sewed together until they were big enough for lap robes. Then they were sent to the hospitals. I tried to make a red one, but it came out crooked and Mama had to unravel it and make it again.

We still couldn't buy much sugar or flour, but eggs went down in price. It was just as well because our chickens had taken to hiding their nests instead of using the nice clean straw in the barn as they were supposed to. Every day when I came home from school, I had to go out and look for hidden nests.

"I should have bought a rooster," said Papa ruefully. "Then we could raise some baby chicks."

"Oh, don't, Sam," begged Mama. "It wouldn't pay, now the price has come down."

"I suppose we could eat them," he suggested, but the way his eyes twinkled I knew he didn't mean it. We couldn't have eaten one of our hens and we didn't. We just kept feeding them and eventually they all died of old age.

Miss Rebecca got over the flu, and although she let Mrs. Barndecker go, she was still pretty weak. She told me to tell Miss Edna that Antoinette could come home now.

"She's your own mother and you must go," Miss Edna told

Antoinette when she looked distressed. "I'll take you there when it's dark enough tonight."

"You stay too," begged Antoinette. "You can have Mrs. Hutchinson's room."

"No thank you," said Miss Edna smiling. "I wouldn't sleep a wink in that old harridan's bed. Besides, you forget I'll be leaving for St. Louis soon."

"Oh," said Antoinette. I could see how disappointed she was and I didn't blame her much. I'd take Miss Edna any day over Miss Rebecca. Miss Edna was like a lion, but poor Miss Rebecca would always be a mouse.

I wanted to go right over to the Hutchinsons after supper, but Mama wouldn't let me.

"You're not family," she reminded me. "This is a family reunion."

"Miss Edna isn't family, either," I reminded her.

"But Edna's been taking care of Antoinette. She'll have to go in for a minute. Now—where did we leave off?"

She picked up *The Last of the Mohicans*, which we were reading aloud, and we all settled down in our usual places before the fireplace. Mama on one side in a rocking chair, me in the middle, and Papa in his Morris chair on the other. He had a bowl of walnuts, which he pried open with his pocket knife, and at the sound of the first shell cracking Caesar came and sat by Papa's knee. Caesar loved walnuts and Papa gave him every third one he cracked.

When the mantle clock bonged nine, Papa, who was reading, finished the sentence, then shut the book with a bang.

"Bedtime," he announced.

But we didn't go to bed just then for there was a knock on the door. It was Miss Edna. Her cheeks were very pink and she was smiling in a way I'd never seen her do before.

"I won't be a minute, but I had to consult you, Judge Burnham."

Papa asked her in and I gave her my chair, but I stood back a ways where I could hear, though not close enough so they would send me to bed.

"You know I'm moving to St. Louis," she began.

"I know," agreed Papa. "Everything's settled. When your house is sold the bank will send you the money. Unless, of course, you've changed your mind."

"Oh no," she said quickly. "I'm going all right. Only Rebecca and Antoinette are coming with me. Can you take care of selling her house and store the way you're doing for me?"

"Rebecca! Moving to St. Louis? Why she said she'd never leave here," said Papa.

"It was all decided tonight," Miss Edna told him. "That little minx of an Antoinette must have planned it. When I told Rebecca I was going to St. Louis, Antoinette asked her mother why didn't they go too. She had it all thought out. We'd get on the train together and just leave."

"What did Rebecca say?" asked Mama curiously.

"At first she said no. She wouldn't know anybody and she'd be scared. But Antoinette said she'd know me, and I would show them what to do."

"Have you ever been in St. Louis?" asked Papa curiously.

"Never. But if other folks manage, I figure I can too. I'll— we'll go to a hotel and get a room. Then I'll call Mrs. Kingery and ask her advice about where to locate my shop."

"If it's right downtown, it's likely to be expensive, Edna," Papa reminded her in a troubled voice.

"I know." For a minute she looked thoughtful. "But Rebecca wants to go in partnership with me. She wants to get a big house, where we can all live together, and a shop downtown." She actually giggled a little. "I think she's think-ing of her father's hardware store. She wants to get out while Antoinette's in school. She doesn't want to sit alone—"

"I should think not," said Mama firmly. "After all those years of living behind walls she should get out and meet people."

"Yes, she should," agreed Miss Edna. "But she won't do it without me. I feel a little like a dog leading a blind person, but she'll get over it. And Antoinette can go to school where nobody knows about her. I wouldn't want her to go through what I did here in Maple Glen. And Rebecca sews very nicely. No style, but with me to do the cutting and fitting—"

"What do you want me to do?" asked Papa. "Seems to me you have it all planned."

"Draw up a contract, making us equal partners in the shop." Miss Edna ticked off the jobs on her fingers. "Rebecca will be Mrs. Hutchinson from now on, not Miss Hutchinson. But I guess you won't need that on the contract."

Papa shook his head.

"Then sell her store and the house. She wants the furniture to go with it. And get somebody to tear down that wicked wall around it. The money can go in the bank, the same as you've arranged for mine and when she gets there she can have it transferred to a bank there."

"Part of it's easy," said Papa. "Ed Brown's been trying to buy the hardware store for years, but the old lady wouldn't sell. As for the house, well, with the wall down maybe some-body may buy it. I've even forgotten what it looks like."

"What about Antoinette? How are they going to explain about her being here?" I was so interested that I'd forgotten about being quiet.

"Go to bed, young lady," ordered Papa in his judge's voice. "I sent you there a half-hour ago."

Chapter 18

IT WASN'T UNTIL THE NEXT DAY that I found out. Papa was going to drive Miss Rebecca and Antoinette to Salem. Antoinette would be hidden under lap robes in the back seat. When they came back, she would be sitting on the seat with Miss Rebecca. They'd tell everybody she was a relative (which was true) and that she was from Seattle (after all she'd been born there). Then they had to tell a white lie and say her parents had died in the flu epidemic and Miss Rebecca, as her only living relative, was going to adopt her.

"Imagine that spineless Rebecca Hutchinson raising a child," said Aunt Gertrude when she heard about it. "Well, at least it's better than an orphanage. I wonder if the child has money."

"I'm sure she'll be no financial strain on Rebecca. Sam says she's well off," said Mama defensively.

"How much do you think?" asked Aunt Gertrude.

But if Mama knew she wouldn't tell. That would have been gossip.

Papa got two men to tear down the wall for the use of the lumber, and they said if they'd known how hard it was going to be they'd never have taken the job. But pretty soon it was finished and the Hutchinson house stood in its big lot for everybody to see. Antoinette was not allowed to go outside because Mrs. Hershy might be looking out of the window.

Finally the day arrived when Miss Rebecca was strong enough to stand the drive to Salem and back. I was in school, but Mama said she was sure they got away without being seen. It was nine o'clock and most of the ladies had gone to the Red Cross with their knitting. Mama called Mrs. Hershy on the telephone and asked for her recipe for angel food cake, since it only took one cup of sugar. Since the Hershys' phone was in the front room, the windows looked the other way so she couldn't see Antoinette get into the back seat of the car and pull the lap robes over her.

I rushed home from school that day, but they weren't back yet. Mama said I made her fidgety with my pacing up and down, so I went over to see Mrs. Hershy.

"Come in. Come in," she urged. "The coffeepot's on the stove, and I've got news you'll never believe!"

We went out into her fragrant-smelling kitchen and she poured two cups of coffee. Mine was only half full to leave room for the cream.

Mrs. Hershy sat down opposite me and her blue eyes fairly twinkled happiness.

"My Ralphie's coming home," she announced. "And that's not all. He's bringing a bride."

"Ralph is married?" I could hardly believe it. What kind of girl would marry that cat-killer anyway?

"Her name was Muriel Smith, and he met her in the Red Cross canteen," continued Mrs. Hershy. "Isn't that romantic? He says she's sort of quiet, but he's sure we'll like her. And we will. Of course, they'll stay here at first, but then he's going to buy a house. Imagine, my Ralphie buying a house. I hope it's not clear at the other end of town."

I had an inspiration.

"Why doesn't he buy the Hutchinson house?" I asked. "Miss Rebecca's going to put it on the market as soon as she leaves. She's selling all the furniture with it."

"Rebecca's leaving?" Her little ball of a nose quivered with excitement and for a minute I felt just terrible. I thought Miss Edna and Miss Rebecca had told everybody, but evidently they hadn't.

"She's traveling," I improvised quickly. "Her cousin—I guess it's her cousin—from Seattle is coming here and then they're going to travel."

"I heard all about that cousin. Must be the family Rebecca stayed with when she run off a long time ago. You know the cousin's name?"

"It's Hutchinson."

"Then that'd be Harry's folks," said Mrs. Hershy quickly. "Phoebe never could abide them. It's a wonder she stayed so long when she went up to fetch Rebecca home. I don't mind saying that Rebecca's got more gumption than I gave her credit for. Traveling that way with a young 'un she don't know."

"She's got Miss Edna to start with." Everybody in Maple Glen would see them leave so I might as well tell this part. "They're taking the same train. At least as far as Portland."

"Phoebe Hutchinson would turn over in her grave if she knew her precious Rebecca was traveling in the company of that woman. Everybody in town knows she's a—knows all about her. You say Rebecca's putting her house up for sale?"

"The house and everything in it." I was relieved that she seemed to be willing to drop the subject of Miss Edna. I was afraid I might have said something I shouldn't.

"It'd be perfect for Ralphie!" cried Mrs. Hershy. "Maybe me and Will could give it to him and his bride for a wedding present. Now that the wall is down, I could keep an eye on her when he was away at work."

Poor Ralphie, I thought, standing up to go. And poor bride. Under Mrs. Hershy's watchful eye they'd have no life of their own. But it served him right for shooting my cat.

Papa got home by dusk. He sat in the front seat alone, while Miss Rebecca and Antoinette sat in back, holding hands. Antoinette looked very pretty. Her hair, when it wasn't strained back in a tight braid, had a tendency to curl. She wore a new coat with a squirrel collar and high galoshes, not just plain rubbers, over her shoes. It seemed strange to hear her call Miss Rebecca "Mama" instead of by her first name. Probably Mrs. Hutchinson had laid down that rule.

"I think I found a buyer for your house," I told them excitedly. "Ralph Hershy. He got married and Mrs. Hershy wants him living close."

Papa groaned.

"Don't just give it away," said Mama sharply. "It could stand a coat of paint, but it's a good house."

"I don't care what it brings," said Miss Rebecca. "I never want to see it again."

Mama had dinner ready for everybody, and while we were eating, Miss Edna arrived. Mama told me to get another plate and silverware, and though she apologized for getting there at mealtime, Miss Edna was persuaded to sit down and eat with us.

"Now the only question is, when do we leave? Everything's in order, Judge."

"The contract's drawn up, and I've got an offer for your house, Edna. It's only a thousand dollars. Your grandpa had a full acre of land there, so if you want to wait maybe I can get more. Ed Brown's signed the papers on the hardware store. He was tickled to death to get it. He'll have to buy on time, but the bank will handle that."

I told Miss Edna then about Ralph Hershy being married. "And Mrs. Hershy wants to buy Miss Rebecca's house as a wedding present for Ralph."

"Well, that's a surprise," said Miss Edna.

"And I've got a surprise, too," said Miss Rebecca shyly. She opened her purse and handed an envelope to Miss Edna.

"Tickets!" exclaimed Miss Edna when she opened it. "Two adults and one child's ticket for St. Louis. But they're marked for next Saturday, and this is Thursday."

"Did I do wrong?" quavered Miss Rebecca. "I didn't see any sense in waiting. I've only my valises to pack and you've been getting ready all week."

"It was my idea," said Antoinette. "I think we should get started." For a minute she sounded a little like her grandmother.

"So do I," agreed Miss Edna instantly. "No, Mrs. Burnham —I mustn't stay for dessert. If we're leaving Saturday I'd better get home and finish sorting things to take."

After they had all gone, I turned to Mama.

"Do you think they'll be happy?"

"Happier than if they stayed here. Sometimes people need a fresh start. And they certainly do. Especially Antoinette."

"It wasn't her fault she was born any more than it was Miss Edna's. People shouldn't hold it against them."

"Someday maybe they won't," said Mama gently. "Think about *The Scarlet Letter* and Hester Prynne. That was less than a hundred years ago. Maybe in another hundred years, or even fifty, people like Edna and Antoinette won't have to hang their heads at all."

"I hope so," I said fervently.

Take a look at these books
by Evelyn Sibley Lampman!